Books by Cynthia Voigt

Building Blocks

BUILDING BLOCKS

by Cynthia Voigt

Atheneum · New York · 1984

LIBRARY OF CONGRESS CATALOGING IN PUBLICATION DATA

Voigt, Cynthia.   *Building blocks.*

SUMMARY: *In a trip back in time, Brann meets his father
as a ten-year-old and learns for the first time to love
and understand him.*
  [*1. Space and time—Fiction.*   *2. Fathers and sons—
Fiction*]   *1. Title.*
PZ7.V874Bu   1984   [*Fic*]   *83-15853*
ISBN 0-689-31035-8

Copyright © 1984 by Cynthia Voigt
All rights reserved
*Published simultaneously in Canada by
McClelland & Stewart, Ltd.*
*Composition by Maryland Linotype,
Baltimore, Maryland*
*Printed and bound by Fairfield Graphics,
Fairfield, Pennsylvania*
Designed by Mary Ahern
First Printing January 1984
Second Printing July 1984

To
WALTER
who built it
and
DUFFLE
who crawled in

Building Blocks

one

THEY were fighting again. Brann lay on the folded-up sofabed in the den/bedroom/TV room and listened. The door was closed, but in this rickety-tickety box of a house you could hear almost anything that went on, whether doors were open or closed.

You'd think, he thought, that on the first day of his summer vacation they could restrain themselves. It was a clear morning in late June. He should be out riding his bike around the neighborhood, and here he was instead, feeling like a lead weight was pressing him down onto the sofa because his parents were fighting. At eight-thirty in the morning.

He should have left the table sooner, but his mother was using her Level One voice, so Brann figured it would all be OK. Besides, the sunlight was lying like a puddle in the middle of the table and his glass of orange juice shone like an undiscovered jewel and it

3

was the first day of vacation—how was he supposed to know it would turn into a Level Two fight?

He should have known, Brann said to himself, listening to the voices from the kitchen (his mother's sharp and angry, quick and final; his dad's low and apologetic). Ever since that letter from the lawyer had come, a big fight had been building. Before then, for almost a month, his mother had been dancing around the house, teasing everybody, because she had scored so high on her law school aptitude test. Number one percentile in the state. In New York that really meant something. She said she only took the test for a lark and a challenge, just to see. She said she knew she couldn't actually go to law school, not yet, not for years; and by then probably she wouldn't be able to get into anywhere good. That didn't matter now. Now she was just glad that she had done so well.

Brann knew that feeling, knowing that you were quicker and smarter than almost everybody else. You felt like you were on top of everyone, like you could do anything. You felt so good about yourself—there was nobody you'd rather be.

Then the letter from the lawyer came, saying that some old cousin in Arizona had died and left a farm to his father. Not a farm in Arizona—that would be a ranch—but in Pennsylvania, near where his father had grown up, over by the Ohio state line. Brann had the same idea his mother had, right away: if they sold the farm, she could quit her job down at Legal Aid and go to law school. His imagination soared away on the possibility. She would be a lawyer, and she'd earn pots of money and they would move into a house where

Brann could have a big room of his own and maybe a swimming pool, but for sure a new ten-speed bike, the kind most of his friends had; and summer camp, too, and enough spending money to have a hamburger whenever he felt like it.

But his father didn't want to sell the farm. He wouldn't say so, not out in the open and clear. His father didn't say things out like that. He just hedged and hummed and said, "Anyway." After he said, "Anyway," he never said anything else. It could drive you crazy. It drove Brann crazy and it drove his mother crazy too.

The fight that morning had started with the farm. They were eating scrambled eggs, with bacon. Brann sat alone in the middle of the table because Sarah was off at the beach for the weekend, and Harry had gone to ROTC summer camp.

Brann's mother had looked up from her last bite of eggs and smiled at Brann. Her bright brown hair (red like his when she had been his age, she said) caught the sunlight; her brown eyes that poured out all her feelings had green flecks in them. She had a sharp face, with dark eyebrows. Harry and Sarah looked like her, except for the dark, thick eyelashes that they got from their father, and the big eyes set deep into their faces. Brann looked like his father, with quiet gray eyes that took things in but didn't let them out. His red hair lay straight and flat, like his father's pale brown hair. Brann's father, Kevin Connell, had a quiet face that didn't give anything away, and a wide, wide mouth that didn't very often smile. They were opposites, his mother and father. She was all short, quick energy, and he was tall and slow and didn't do much. Brann's mother poured her personality out, all over the house so you couldn't get away from it. His dad didn't say much, and you never knew what he was thinking, except that his wide mouth made you feel like whatever it was, it wasn't too exciting. Brann felt like he was his father on the outside and his mother on the inside. He wondered why they had married one another. Especially, he wondered why she had wanted to marry him.

This Saturday morning, Brann was sitting there feeling good about summer all stretched out ahead of him, and his mother asked his father: "Why did she leave it to you? She had children of her own."

"You know why, Diane," Brann's father answered. "There was more than enough money and she knew Uncle Andrew wanted me to have it. He said so, he said if it worked out he'd like me to get the farm. That's what the letter says."

"Why would he do that? What about his own children?"

"Both of his sons died in the war," Brann's father repeated the tired information. "His daughters weren't interested."

"But still—"

"And I guess he had a good idea of how much I liked it," Brann's father said. "Maybe he wanted to give me something, maybe—he was my godfather too."

"All you did was work there when you were little," she continued.

"I was happy there, and I guess he knew that. When they told me I couldn't go back for summers any more—I don't remember a worse time. Ever." His voice faded away, as if he had changed his mind about saying something more. Brann felt a flicker of curiosity about what his father had been going to say. The flicker died away, because it probably wasn't interesting anyway.

Brann's mother waited for a minute, then made an impatient gesture with her hand.

"No, I mean it, Di. Remember when we had to put Victor down?"

Brann guessed his mother remembered. He sure did. Victor was old and smelly and had cataracts in both eyes and could barely get out the door to make his messes he was so weak and arthritic. They knew they had to have him put to sleep. Nobody wanted to do it. Brann's father had dropped Brann and his mother off at a Saturday matinee—*Blazing Saddles*—and Brann remembered they'd laughed more than the movie was funny. When they got back home, his dad had taken care of everything, even wrapping old Victor up and burying him over by the little garden patch. Brann and his mother were still laughing about that movie. Brann knew that he was laughing because if he didn't he'd be bawling and making useless protests and thinking about things he didn't want to think about. He didn't know why his mother was laughing. He hadn't wanted to hear anything about Victor, and his dad hadn't told him anything. His dad just looked at his mother and said, "It's all done, Di." His mother had said "Thank you," and then, surprising Brann, "I'm sorry, Kev." His dad just asked them about the movie. That was last fall, a long time gone. But what did Victor have to do with this farm?

His mother asked, "What does that have to do with the farm?"

"I felt the same way, when they told me."

"But that was years ago. You never went back. How can you say you liked it so much if you never went back?"

"I felt too bad about it to go back."

Brann looked at his father. He knew that he himself avoided going out onto that part of their little yard where Victor was. Wasn't. But why should his father feel so bad about an old farm?

"That's all years in the past anyway. What does it matter now?" Brann's mother asked impatiently.

Brann's father shrugged, and he looked away.

"The place must be worth thousands now," she insisted.

"I guess maybe."

"More than enough—we can't expect Sarah to get a scholarship, Kev, and there's Brann coming along—"

"Hey!" Brann protested. "I'm only twelve. Much too young to start worrying about college. Don't drag me into this."

His father looked at him with those thick-lashed, gray eyes. For a minute, Brann wondered what he was thinking, and then abandoned it. What his father thought didn't matter, since he never did anything about his ideas.

"And I could start law school in the fall. I can't go to law school part time like I did NYU, Kev—"

"I know, Diane."

"It isn't as if I've ever asked you for anything before. I always paid my own tuition—"

"I know."

"And kept the house and managed to live within the budget—laundry, insurance, meals—driving the kids around—doctors and dentists and parties—"

"I know, Diane." Brann's father seemed to get flatter and flatter at his end of the table. Brann drank his juice down at one gulp and stood up.

"And now when there's a chance—I could succeed, Kev, you know I could. I could compete and succeed. You don't. You don't even try."

"It's fate, Di," Brann's father said. Brann put his dishes in the sink. When his father said, "It's fate," a big argument was going to begin. His father always said that, "It's fate," as if that should end all trying. Those were his giving-up words, as if fate came and wrapped around you like a huge feather pillow. Brann could feel his mother beginning to get steamed. He walked out of the kitchen, through the narrow living room, and closed the door of the den/bedroom/TV room behind him.

"You never try," his mother said, her voice rising.

"I've stuck to my job—"

"A job you never liked. That's not sticking. That's inertia. Drawing the fronts for development houses . . ." Brann could hear the quality of his mother's scorn. "Don't try to tell me you're satisfied with yourself."

"I don't," his father said. "I'm not." That was true, Brann thought, listening from under the lead weight. His dad didn't lie about things.

"But that's *your* problem, and I've stopped trying to solve it for you. It's your life and if at forty-seven that's the way you want to be, go ahead and I'm not

9

feeling sorry for you." She began to bang dishes around in the sink. "But I'm almost forty and this is 1974—and I care about *my* life, I care about *me*, about not being trapped. I can't spring *your* trap, but I can spring mine. I've done your laundry for twenty years and you haven't done one damn thing more than you've had to. You owe it to me, Kevin."

Brann got up off the sofa. He didn't feel like going outside. He opened the den/bedroom/TV room door and slipped into the living room.

"I'm sorry, Di," his father said, low and helpless. "Anyway. I try. It's just the way I am. It's fate. I've never stood in your way."

"You never helped either." His mother had her back to the room. Brann could hear the angry tears in her voice. They would be rolling down her face. Why didn't his father do something? Why was he always shambling around doing the same things over and over making people ashamed? "And now, when you could really help me—"

Brann opened the cellar door. He flicked on the light. From the cellar you couldn't hear anything.

"Just for once in your life *do* something!" his mother cried.

Brann closed the door and hurried down the stairs. If they got a divorce it would be easier. Sarah, wise at seventeen, said that too. Everybody's parents got divorced and it felt strange for a while but you got used to it, Sarah said. Harry, going to college on an ROTC scholarship, just ignored things.

Brann knew that if his mother threw his father out

of the house his father would go. His father always did what his mother said to do. She hammered at him and hammered at him in her angers, and his father would inevitably do whatever it was. He'd sell this farm eventually; but by then it would be an old poison in all of them. Why couldn't he just sell it right away? Why did he have to pretend to himself that he wasn't going to give in?

The cellar had concrete floors and concrete walls. There were two rooms down there, a laundry room, which had the furnace in it, and a smaller storeroom, where his father's tools and worktable were.

Brann pulled on the overhead light in this small room and closed the door behind him. The yellow light shone bright. He couldn't hear anything. The room was a little sack of silence, hanging off the bottom of the unhappy house.

Brann stood before the high worktable and fiddled with his father's tools, kept there in neat rows. He flipped through the stack of artist's notebooks piled up at one side. He found the design for Sarah's dollhouse and for all the furniture in it; the plan for Harry's wooden train set, which was now packed away in a big box in another corner of the room, behind the blocks Kevin Connell had played with as a boy, which all of his own children had played with in their time. Brann had just outgrown them a year ago and they, too, were stored down here.

Brann flipped pages to look at designs for houses to be built on mountainsides and for clusters of apartment buildings to front onto a large central park. His father had ideas, no doubt of it—he just never did anything about them. There were drawings too, and Brann studied one of the four Connells, his mother and three kids, done when Brann was three. In the picture they were sitting out in the country somewhere, under a tree. He could almost smell the summer air in that one. He had forgotten the actual day, but the picture made it realer to him than memory could. His dad sure could draw, Brann thought. But being talented didn't help anything, not unless you tried for something with your talent.

"It's fate," his father said. Well, Brann had done some thinking about fate. Who wouldn't, in this century? With overpopulation so bad they were all liable to starve, and even Brann—who was one of the lucky ones, who lived in a good neighborhood in a rich country—could see ten matchbox houses from his front door, crowded together along the street. With pollution in the air. And pollution in the waters, spreading like some horrible disease, like the black plague crossing continents, killing lakes and rivers. And pollution in government, with this Watergate thing, which stank as far as Brann was concerned. Billy Whitcomb's father, a reporter with the *Times* with his own by-line, said the same thing. And at any minute bombs could drop and blow everything to kingdom come. Who wouldn't think about fate?

You shouldn't lie there and let fate smother you. You should charge out to meet it. In all the stories Brann had read, the people had taken hold of their own fates, grabbed onto them. Alexander, King Arthur, Napoleon —they didn't use fate as an excuse for not doing anything. Even when they knew it was a bad fate, they went after it. Fate was like a sword blade, hard and sharp.

Brann slammed his hand down on the table. He hit it so hard his palm stung, and the old sketch his dad kept tacked on the wall over the worktable rattled in its five-and-dime frame. Aunt Rebecca, his father's youngest sister. Aunt Rebecca was the only one in his whole big family that Brann's father liked; but he liked her enough for all the rest put together. She lived in Taiwan with her husband, who was a pilot, so they never saw her. But it was Rebecca Brann's father talked about on the rare occasions when he talked about his childhood, and Brann felt like he knew her, between that and her frequent letters. In the drawing, she was a kid, about ten, laughing and about to start running somewhere. She didn't care where as long as it was someplace new. She'd make it an exciting place, just by being there. Brann's Aunt Rebecca had the same wide mouth his father and Brann had, but on her it was beautiful, because her smile was so big, because she was so happy.

The fight upstairs would go on for a while, then his father would wander helplessly around the house for a while, or maybe go outside and stake the tomato plants he'd put in along the back of the little plot of yard. The Connells lived here, in this township where all the houses were overpriced, for the sake of the school system. It was supposed to be one of the best public school systems in the country. His father had to commute into the city to go to work, an hour a day each way on the train, and that was expensive too.

Everything was expensive, everything was too

expensive here, but the school system was worth the sacrifices. They said. Brann didn't care. He wasn't about to care about anything.

If things were different. If, for example, he had a father like Billy Whitcomb's who had his own by-line in the *Times* so people listened to what he had to say. Or even Marty Eliot's, who talked all the time about how great he was and was pretty much of a horse's ass, but made a lot of money doing nose jobs and face lifts. The Eliots went for vacations to places like Squaw Valley and the Virgin Islands. Or a father in the military or who ran his own business, anything, just something Brann could respect. He was the kind of kid who would do better with a father he could be proud of. He wasn't asking for anything impossible, he wasn't asking for a father he liked or anything. But he guessed he was doomed to be the kind of kid who was ashamed of his old man—and it didn't do any good trying to hide it from himself. This kind of truth was like fate, you had to grab hold of it even if it was sharp and painful.

He turned around in the little room, trying to find something to do for a while.

The blocks were built up into the fortress design his father sometimes made. What about a grown man who still played with building blocks? Although these *were* special: old, oak blocks grown golden with the oils of the many hands that had built things with them. Every time you touched them, his father had explained, a little oil from your skin worked into the wood, a little part of yourself got permanently added to them. Most of the deep golden color belonged to his father, who had built with them the most. His dad's Uncle Andrew had made them for his godson, and it was the best set of blocks Brann had ever seen. There were hundreds of them, some as big as bricks, some as small as regular square alphabet blocks, some rounded so you could make pillars, and some curved so you could make arched gateways or windows. You could build just about anything out of those blocks.

Brann crouched down to peer into the enclosure his father had built. He could crawl under the gateway, if he was careful and kept his back low, it was that big. A tower rose out of the center, with a window like a single eye in it. If Brann took that down and built up a shorter tower at each corner, then he could crawl inside the fortress.

He didn't think about it, he just stood up to dismantle the tall tower, carefully, block by block. Then, using the same octagonal design his father had used, he built towers on each corner of the wall, where soldiers would be stationed to keep watch. The wood in his hands felt warm, as if it was touching him as much as he was touching it. It felt familiar. It should, for all the hours he'd played with these blocks.

Sarah would be home tomorrow, and she'd stay home for two weeks before she went off with the family she was going to work for, taking care of their kids for a summer on Cape Cod. She could stop the fights. She just said, "Stuff it you two. Save it for later." So Brann could count on two weeks of peace. Brann reminded himself to go apply again for a paper route that afternoon. You had to go in about once a month, to remind them you were alive, so that when a route opened up you'd get it. With that and his grass-cutting jobs, he might earn fifteen dollars a week. By the end of the summer, he could afford a ten-speed bike—unless prices went up again. And they surely would.

Brann's watchtowers were slender and had many windows, one at each place where the stairs would turn, if there were real stairs inside. He made crenellated tops to them, so the archer sentry could fire off warning shots. Crossbows, he corrected himself; these soldiers would be armed with crossbows. His father's tower had had solidity and grace, both. Brann's towers didn't look the way they had looked in his imagination. They never did. His father knew without thinking what shape belonged where, and how wide the base had to be for it to narrow up to the right-sized top. Brann's father would have built these towers slowly, but Brann was a fast worker.

His father knew a lot of things, like how to build cabinets and put in electric wiring. He just didn't *do* things—except the lousy draftsman job where he'd always worked, an architectural factory he called it, a long room with tables in it, and everybody drawing on them at once. Other men quit or got promoted, but not Brann's father. He didn't try for things. He didn't even stick up for things.

About the only thing Brann knew his father had stuck up for, had demanded and gotten, was the naming of Brann. Brann's mother told the story, and Brann could never tell how she felt about it. She was used to getting her own way, but Brann suspected she liked having his father win an argument, because she only told the story when she was feeling good.

Before Brann was born, they'd decided that he should be named after his father's side of the family. If he was a boy he'd be Thomas, after his father's father. If he was a girl, he'd be Rebecca of course. But he was a boy and his dad was sitting beside his mother in the hospital when they brought him in—eight pounds eleven ounces, screaming for food; with a head of red hair, they said, waving his arms and legs, and completely out of temper with the world. The nurse brought the birth certificate to fill out. His father suddenly said, "Brann, with two n's."

"*What?*" his mother said. She put all the surprise in her voice every time she told the story. "What was I to think?" she would ask them, "a child of mine who was supposed to have the perfectly sensible name of Thomas turned into something you'd expect to find in a supermarket, next to Whole Wheat or All-Purpose." Remembering, Brann grinned—he liked the way his mother told stories.

"That's his name," his father had said.

"What do you mean? What about Thomas?"

Meanwhile, baby Brann was howling away. They were ignoring him.

"I don't know. It just—came to me. No, honestly, Di, I don't know. But that's his name. I choose it. No arguments, not about this."

His mother said she flapped her mouth a couple of times, then gave in. "I was still pretty weak," she said. "He took advantage of my weakness."

Brann wasn't sure how he felt about her giving in. He always had to introduce himself, Brann with two n's Connell. It was an odd name, and he didn't like that. Teachers always asked him what kind of name it was, and he would say what his father said, "It's Irish." But it sure was unusual, and Brann liked that. He also liked his father arguing up for it.

The towers were finished. He sat back on his heels to study the effect. In general it was all right, but the towers didn't rise high enough. They couldn't be any higher, but they could look higher. His dad would know how to do that.

Brann crawled inside the fortress. There was room to sit cross-legged in it, even room to curl up on the floor. He heard footsteps overhead. Somebody looking for him. Let her look, let him look. If they didn't care any more about him than to ruin the first day of his vacation with that kind of fighting—let them worry. Serve them right. He had enough worries just being alive without adding their problems to it and having to listen and wishing his father would just tell her to shut her mouth. But his father never did that, and he never would do that, because Brann's mother was right about it all, right about everything. Except marrying his father.

Brann curled up a little more tightly, careful not to knock against the wall with his bare feet, and fell asleep.

two

I T WAS dark when Brann woke up. Somebody must have come down and turned off the light. There wasn't even (he peered through the broad gateway which led into his father's fortress) a line of light under the door to the laundry room. He wondered how long he'd slept there on the cool cement floor.

(The floor wasn't cool, wasn't cement.)

He could see the vague shape of the fortress gateway even here in the absolute night of the windowless cellar room.

(The floor was wood.)

Brann jerked awake and sat up without thinking. Around him, building blocks exploded, clattered and banged on a wooden floor. That was strange. He must still be asleep.

He heard a movement across the darkness, like sheets rustling, or a mattress creaking. He looked in that direction.

A window gleamed under a night sky. So he was dreaming he was in a room. He could see the top branches of a tree, black against the sky. The branches swayed slightly, in leafy moonlight. Brann's eyes grew accustomed to the dim light. He looked around the room: a bureau with a mirror on top of it, a door opposite the window, a bed beside the window, and a boy sitting up in the bed, staring at him. What kind of a dream was this? The boy's hair was cropped short and he had a long face, pale in the moonlight, with dark eyes in the middle of it. The boy stared and stared at Brann. Brann stared and stared back, waiting for the dream to take its direction.

Nothing happened.

The silence mounted. Brann moved cautiously to pinch himself, hard. It hurt.

But it shouldn't hurt—when you pinched yourself in dreams it wasn't supposed to hurt. And in dreams you couldn't move your body the way you usually could. As soon as he thought of that, Brann stood up.

If he was awake, what was going on? He couldn't be awake.

"Who are you?" the boy in the bed asked. He didn't move. "Where did you come from?" His voice was low and whispery, scared.

"New York," Brann said. His own voice sounded high and squeaky. He jammed his hands into his blue-jean pockets. You could dream you were awake. He'd done that. "Where do *you* come from?"

"I live here," in the same voice. "What are you doing in my room?"

"I fell asleep." Brann whispered too. "Why are you whispering?"

"My grandparents are down the hall. Grandma sleeps lightly. I'm surprised you didn't wake her up knocking over the blocks. How'd you get into our house?"

Brann shrugged. Really, it had to be a dream. It would explain itself, sooner or later. He waited to see what the frightened little kid would do next.

"What's your name?"

"Brann, with two n's."

"Are you a burglar?"

Brann decided to take the offensive in this conversation. "Are you scared of burglars?"

"No." The boy shook his head. "My father would take care of them good. Besides, we haven't got anything to steal. Unless they're tramps and just hungry—but then they'd stick to the kitchen, if they got in." He was a skinny kid, and little in his bed.

"How old are you?" Brann asked.

"Ten. Almost ten-and-a-half. How old are you?"

"Twelve."

"You're going into seventh grade. I bet you can do long division."

"Easy," Brann said. "That's kid stuff. At my school we have to learn everything, like all the Presidents—"

"I know who the President is, it's Roosevelt. Franklin Delano Roosevelt again. My father voted for him, both times. My mother didn't the first time but she did last fall. Who did your father vote for?"

"I don't know," Brann lied. He was busy remembering Social Studies classes: if it was Roosevelt and his second term, it had to be the Depression. This was about the weirdest dream he'd ever had. If there was a weird dream contest, this one was a sure winner. He did know who his father had voted for: McGovern. His father had backed the loser.

"Do you know how many states there are?" the boy asked.

"Fifty."

"Nope, forty-eight. What's the capital of this state?"

"Albany," Brann said.

"Nope, Harrisburg."

Harrisburg? But Harrisburg was the capital of Pennsylvania. Now Brann knew a little more, like another block put into place. The boy sat on his bed looking smug. "What's the capital of California?" Brann asked.

"San Francisco?"

"Naw, Sacramento. Connecticut?"

"New Haven."

"No, Hartford." The kid didn't look smug any more. "Anyway, what's your name?"

"Kevin. What did you say yours was?"

"Brann with two n's."

"That's a funny name."

"It's Irish," Brann explained.

"My father's part Irish," the boy said. "Do you want to come over here and sit on the bed? You still haven't said what you're doing here. You can't stay anyway, if he catches you. Don't knock over any more blocks. What are you doing here?"

"Waiting to wake up," Brann answered. He picked his way carefully among fallen blocks. The bed creaked when he sat on it.

Kevin studied him, like a mouse looking at a snake. Brann wondered what the dream was going to be about. "Are you a runaway? I've read about runaway kids, but the papers say they go in gangs. That was a joke, wasn't it? About waking up? Want me to pinch you?"

Brann nodded, and the boy pinched him gently on the arm. "Harder," Brann said. But it was no use. He was dreaming he was awake in Pennsylvania somewhere, during the Great Depression. He didn't feel like he was dreaming, he felt like he was awake. But that was impossible. "Never mind," Brann said. He was asleep. He had to be. Impossible things didn't happen. "What time is it?"

"Late," the boy said. "You can't stay here."

"I know," Brann said. "You don't have to tell me that. I don't want to anyway." He heard two long whistles, like boat signals. But Pennsylvania didn't border on the ocean.

"I don't know what my father would say—he'd probably whip you or turn you over to the police, or both. He'd whip me too. He has a belt. It hurts; nothing hurts as much. So you've got to go."

"Is the ocean near here?" Brann asked. Sometimes in dreams you couldn't wake yourself up, no matter how hard you tried. You had to wait for things to get scary enough to wake you up. But he wasn't scared. If anyone was scared it was this Kevin kid, huddling in the bed with his sheet pulled up to his shoulders.

"The river, the Ohio River. I've never seen the ocean."

"How am I supposed to get out?" Brann asked.

"How'd you get in?"

"I flew in the window," Brann said. He giggled. In dreams wasn't that how you traveled, with your arms spread out, floating? "So I'll just fly out." That would prove it for sure.

"That's not funny," the boy said. "Did you come up the back stairs to the second floor and then up here? It's lucky you came to *my* room. If Grandma had seen you—she's old and her heart's not good. Grandpa is deaf, so nothing bothers him. Can you find your way down all right?"

"No," Brann said. "Because I didn't come in, come up." He was beginning to get scared. He tried to keep fear out of his voice, but the boy heard it.

"You've done something wrong, haven't you?" Kevin asked. Brann shook his head, then nodded it. He didn't know. "And you don't want to talk about it."

Brann nodded again. How could he say, *I fell asleep and when I woke up I wasn't where I'd been to fall asleep, and I think this is all a dream but it feels too real to be a dream. If it isn't a dream that means I've maybe traveled through time; but that's impossible.*

Kevin's eyes took in everything about Brann. "Well," he finally said, "I could take you out to the garage. You could sleep there. Maybe you could have breakfast with us. If you wanted to. Anyway. But you better think up a good story, because my mother is pretty sharp with strangers. If she thinks something's fishy, I'll tell her just what happened. I don't want to get whipped."

"OK," Brann said. Dreams could seem awfully real, he reminded himself.

They slipped off the bed. Kevin was sleeping in his underpants, just like an ordinary kid. Brann pushed his feet down on the floor so hard the contact jarred up his ankles; but he still didn't wake up.

Kevin moved silently across the room and Brann followed as silently on bare feet. The boy opened the door and looked out. A light went on. With one hand Kevin pushed Brann back into the room. "Don't move," he hissed, as if their lives depended on it. Brann stood with his back flat against the wall, his heart beating in his ears, listening.

He heard shuffling footsteps, then an airy voice: "Kevin? Is that you? I thought I heard voices."

Kevin stepped out into the hallway. "It's just me, Grandma."

"I heard a noise, and then voices. But I thought I might be dreaming and you know how they go on if I wake them up. I listened. I tried to go back to sleep. It was whispering. Did you hear whispering?" The voice sounded urgent.

"I heard it, Grandma, don't worry. It was me. I got up and ran into the blocks. I knocked the whole building down, then I was talking to myself."

"Why?"

"It was dark. I was lonely. I'm going downstairs

now and get a glass of water so you'll hear that. I'll be coming upstairs again, so you'll hear that too. Don't worry."

The two voices were receding, as if the speakers were walking away.

"I have never walked in my sleep," the airy voice declared.

"I know, Grandma."

"Nor snored."

"Well now, I don't think that's true."

"I knew you'd tell the truth. You're a good boy, Kevin."

"I'm going to turn out the hall light."

"That's nice."

Brann waited a brief moment in darkness, then stepped into the doorway. Kevin grabbed his arm and they moved together down a dark hall. "Stairs," Kevin whispered into Brann's ear, "eighteen." He kept a light grip on Brann's arm.

Brann stepped out into darkness and counted eighteen steps down, bare wood. On the lower floor the hallway was carpeted. Kevin crept along the hall at a snail's pace, his hand now painfully tight on Brann's arm.

"Down ten, then a landing, down another twenty." The words were breathed into Brann's ear. Brann could feel the tenseness in the boy's body.

But why was Kevin scared? It was his own house. Kevin was more scared even than Brann, and Brann was moving around in darkness in a place he'd never seen before.

They crossed the ground floor. Brann saw dark, hulking shapes of furniture, dark doorways, and lighter window panes. He didn't think, he just followed the boy beside him. They stepped out onto a small porch and down five steps to a cement walk. It was lighter outside, and Brann saw Kevin's face white in the moonlight.

"Grandma's getting senile," Kevin said. "It was after her stroke last winter. But it scares her when she can't remember things, or hears things that aren't there. It scares her when there's—an uproar. It's dangerous for her to be scared because if she has another stroke she'll probably die."

"My grandfather got senile," Brann said, to show that he sympathized. "But I never knew what it meant. I was too little, and they put him in a home. Your grandmother doesn't seem bad. I wonder why they put my grandfather away?"

"Away?"

"In a nursing home. They didn't let kids visit. I can't remember him at all. I only ever had one grandmother."

"Why?"

"My other one, my father's mother, died when he was young."

The night was warm, with a faint breeze to rustle the leaves of the trees. The humidity was high so the air hung close.

"That's the garage. There's a side door."

"Is it locked?"

"Why should it be locked?"

A long, hooting sound slid through the dark air, coiling like a snake. Then Brann heard the train rushing along behind it. "Are you coming with me?"

Kevin shook his head. He was scared to go with Brann. He was littler than Brann, so Brann tried to be understanding; but he didn't feel understanding. Brann didn't want to go on alone into that dark place. He didn't want to be left alone. "What about tomorrow?" he asked, to keep the other boy's company a little longer.

"I don't know."

"Could you find me and take me inside? As if you just found me?"

"What'll you tell them?"

"Who? Your parents? Can we tell them I go to your school?"

"They could find out it's not true."

"Do they know everybody in your school?"

"I don't know. Brann? Maybe you should go somewhere else."

"But I can't, not tonight. Where else could I go?" But in a dream, you went places without traveling. Brann sighed. He would get no help from this kid. "I'll take care of it. I'll think of something."

"I guess so," the boy said reluctantly.

It has to be a dream, Brann announced to himself. He stepped out confidently, without looking back, as he would in a dream.

Kevin didn't wait to see what happened. Brann heard him scuttering back toward the house.

Brann walked up to the low, dark building and turned the knob on the door. It opened easily. A truck was parked inside, an old-fashioned pickup with slatted sides to its back section and a rounded hood. The one-car garage smelled of gas and oil. The truck had a running board.

Brann gave himself extra credit for details in this dream and pulled down on the door handle. He climbed up onto the seat. Cloth, not plastic. He leaned against the door and shifted his body until it was comfortable.

He concentrated, the way he often did when he wanted to fall asleep, on pretending he was the son of someone else, imagining what his life would be like. The sooner he got to sleep the sooner he would wake up in his own house.

WHEN he opened his eyes, faint sunlight filtered into the garage. His neck was stiff, his T-shirt was drenched with sweat, and a boy was staring at him through the curved windshield of an old-fashioned truck.

Brann couldn't think. He couldn't speak. He stared at the boy without seeing him. On television, in science fiction shows or "The Twilight Zone," they showed people being whirled down dark tunnels—arms and legs spread out—down and away. They didn't show people just . . . waking up.

It wasn't a dream. It had to be a dream but it wasn't. He knew that now, for sure. He was somewhere out in time (which wasn't possible), and he had no idea how he'd gotten there. So he had no idea how to get back. (But that was impossible, really impossible. Impossible things didn't happen.) Dream or not—and it couldn't be a dream, he had to go to the bathroom. It wasn't a dream. He didn't belong anywhere or to anyone, lost out here in time. He was absolutely alone.

And free, with nobody to make claims or tell him what to do, or suck him into their unhappy quarrels. The only person who knew who he was was this kid with his dark-fringed gray eyes and his broad, scared, fish mouth. And even he didn't know anything about Brann.

It was scary, dark and windy scary. It was also exciting. An adventure, some adventure back in time. It was crazy. Brann grinned. The boy smiled tentatively back at him. Brann opened the door to the truck and climbed out.

"I thought you might have gone," Kevin said. He wore a pair of denim overalls without a shirt.

"So did I," Brann said. His brain felt dizzy. "But I guess I'm still here. Sorry about that. It's fate I guess."

"What does that mean, it's fate?"

"Fate? It's what has to happen and you can't fight it. What time's it? Where am I anyway?"

"Nearly seven. You're in our garage," Kevin answered. He looked worried.

"I *know* that about the garage," Brann didn't bother to keep the sarcasm out of his voice. "What's the name of the town?"

"Sewickley," Kevin said. His eyes were on the floor. Brann knew that he had hurt the boy's feelings, but he didn't much care.

"I'm hungry and I've gotta go to the bathroom," Brann said. When somebody was this easy to boss, you couldn't do anything but bully him. "What's the name of a street where your parents wouldn't know who moved in, or be likely to meet them."

"Second Street," Kevin said.

"Don't worry, kid," Brann clapped him on the shoulder. What was the matter with this kid anyway? "Nobody'll get you in trouble." If this kid thought he had problems, he should try on the situation Brann was in. "Lead me inside. If I don't pee, I'll bust."

They went around the truck, which was piled with copper pipes and coiled wires, and out of the smell of gasoline into the fresh air.

Kevin's house stood on a large lot, one among a row of houses that faced an asphalt road. They were all big, square, three-story houses, and they all had big lawns with tall trees growing around them. "What's your father do?" Brann asked.

"He's a builder. He builds houses or kitchens or fixes roofs—whatever people want."

"Nice house," Brann remarked. It was huge.

"It's my grandfather's, we just live here," Kevin said. "We came here after the Depression started. Before that, we lived on the other side of Pittsburgh, close to the mills. That's where my father worked before he lost his job." He was hesitating before the first step up to the back door.

Brann gave him a little shove. "Let's go. Buck up —I've got a plan. All you have to do is introduce me. After you show me the bathroom."

The bathroom was at the end of a narrow hallway, just a toilet and sink. Brann peed and then washed his hands and face. His stomach growled: he was hungry too, good and hungry. He looked at himself in the mirror. He slicked down his hair and met his own eyes. Little lights were dancing in his eyes. He looked like he was enjoying himself, he thought, and then realized that he was. He was eager to find out what the adventure that awaited him was going to be.

Kevin had waited by the door. He led Brann into the kitchen.

The big kitchen had a long table covered with a red-and-white checked oilcloth, a six-burner gas stove, and an old-fashioned refrigerator with one of those round cooling units sitting on top of it. The table was set for eight people, forks, knives, cloth napkins, two plates with butter on them, five glasses of milk and three empty cups. A woman stood with her back to them, working at the stove. She ladled batter from a big bowl onto a griddle that covered half the stove. She piled up the finished pancakes on a platter near the griddle. She wore a flowered dress and sneakers. Her body was square, thick. Her hair looked faded, grays and whites and yellows and maybe a shade of carrot color. She whipped up the batter with strong arms.

"Mom?" Kevin said.

"Get down the Karo and the honey," she answered without turning around. Kevin hurried over to a cupboard.

"I've got someone with me," he said, reaching down two glass jars.

"What? Speak up why don't you?"

"I've got someone here."

She turned around then and saw Brann. He saw that she was pregnant, and younger than he'd thought. Her body was all swollen out and heavy, her face above it was thin and gray looking, tired looking. She looked older than she was, Brann decided. Her eyes were bright blue, and her eyebrows were pale red.

"Who are you?"

"I came to see Kevin," he answered. She put a hand on her hip and looked at him. "I know Kevin from school and I came by," Brann said.

"Have you eaten breakfast?" she asked.

"No, ma'am."

"Set a place for him," she told Kevin, "then call your sisters and brothers and your grandma." She looked back to Brann. "My husband likes breakfast at seven sharp and everyone seated and ready. Go wash your hands."

"But—" Brann began, but she had turned her back to him, so he went back to the bathroom and washed his hands again. She was not the kind of woman you disobeyed, or talked back to. Kevin was at the table when he got back, and Brann slipped into a chair beside the younger boy. He put his napkin in his lap and waited.

The chairs filled up with a tumbling of feet and bodies. Brann was introduced in turn to each person: an ugly little girl in overalls, Suzanne; twins, a boy and a girl, who looked like first graders, Billy and Hannah; the littlest, a boy named Stevie, still a toddler, who climbed up onto the telephone directory on his chair. Last, an old woman, her hair white and wispy, her blue eyes faded and fearful, shuffled in. She wore a cotton bathrobe, tied around her waist.

Kevin's mother put two large platters of pancakes on the table, then sat down heavily at one end. As soon as she did that, Kevin hopped up and poured coffee into his mother's cup, into his grandmother's, and into the cup by the empty place at the head of the table. The little kids squirmed and nudged one another to get more room. Stevie reached out for his milk glass, but his mother stopped his hand with a sharp glance.

Nobody touched anything on the table. Brann looked around and wondered what was going on.

"Quiet now." Kevin's mother spoke. All of the children sat straight and silent.

Brann heard heavy footsteps on the stairs, across floors, and a man entered the kitchen, a big man. He wore an undershirt, the kind with shoulder straps, and cotton workpants. His unfastened belt hung down from the waist of his trousers. He had heavy laced boots on his feet. He stood at the table and said "Morning" into the air above the platters of pancakes. He was answered by a vague murmur of voices; nobody spoke out clearly, as if nobody wanted to be noticed. Certainly Brann felt uncomfortable, and the last thing he wanted was this man to notice him. He looked like the kind of man you hoped wouldn't see you before you had time to get away.

Kevin's father was hairy. He had thick, dark hair on his head and thick hair growing all over his chest, his shoulders and arms, down to the backs of his hands and up over the first knuckles of his fingers. He was thickly built and muscular. His neck was thick. The flesh on his face was thick and leathery, like something formed roughly out of clay and left unfinished. His little gray eyes sat under heavy overhanging eyebrows.

Without a word, without looking at anyone, he

sat down and picked up his fork. He speared a stack of pancakes, buttered them, and poured Karo over them. As soon as he had started eating, everybody else began to grab for pancakes. Kevin cut Stevie's into bite-sized pieces. Kevin's mother put two pancakes on his grandmother's plate, as if she couldn't serve herself.

Nobody spoke. The only sounds in the room were chewing and cutting and the slurping sound of milk. Hungry as he was, Brann ate carefully, using his best manners. He kept his eyes down, trying to be inconspicuous.

When Kevin's father had finished eating, he got up to pour himself another cup of coffee. He didn't return to the table, but stood by the stove surveying the people sitting down, like a general looking over his armies. "Who's this?" he asked, his voice suspicious and unfriendly.

Somebody was going to have to answer him. Nobody wanted to because he wasn't going to like the answer.

Brann didn't look up.

"Polly?" Kevin's father asked.

"It's a friend of Kevin's," she apologized. "He came by and I asked him to eat with us."

There was a silence. Brann couldn't have raised his eyes if his life had depended on it. He sat there.

"What's your name, boy?"

He didn't have to look around to see who had to answer that question: "Brann. With two n's."

"Funny name. That your last name?"

"No, Smith is." Smith was the safest name he'd been able to think of.

"I've never seen you before." The words held threats. "Nor heard about you, Brann Smith."

Brann heard the distrust, and his fear of being found out was greater than his fear of the man. He hoped his time-travel adventure wasn't to do battle with him, he hoped the man wasn't a dragon it was his job to slay. He flicked his eyes up and met the little, assessing gray eyes. He's only a man, nothing special, Brann said to himself. "We're new to Sewickley. We just moved in a couple of weeks ago."

"Say 'sir' when you speak to me."

"Yes, sir."

"What's your father do?" Kevin's father asked Brann.

"He's a draftsman, and he does carpenter work," Brann said. "Sir."

"Who's he with?"

"Nobody, not right now," Brann said, remembering his Social Studies lessons about the Great Depression, when it was likely that a boy's father would be out of work. "He's looking for a job."

"Making cabinets?"

"Any kind of work," Brann said, adding quickly, "sir."

"Where's your family live?"

"On Second Street."

The man nodded, his face showing no expression. He took a big swig of coffee. "If he's good enough, and handy enough—tell him to come see me. But only if he's good enough, mind. I'm easy to find. All you have to do is ask for Thomas Connell."

Brann nodded. The name sat like a lump halfway

down his throat. He thought for a second his breakfast was going to come up.

"I might have something for him. If he'll work long and hard, I could use another man. I never missed a payroll, all these years. Tell him that too."

"Yes sir." Brann managed to get the words past the lump.

"You'll do the books today," Mr. Connell told his wife. She nodded, her hand rubbing at a spot on the tablecloth. "I'll expect lunch around noon, I'll come back to the office for it. Your brother-in-law's dropping by this evening, remember, so the children better be fed early. Uncle Andrew's just coming to talk," Mr. Connell said to Kevin, "so don't get your hopes up." He turned and left the room. Brann heard the screen door slam behind him.

Doors were opening in his mind. Thomas Connell. Suzanne and Hannah and Stevie—Billy was killed in the Korean War. And Kevin Connell.

The boy sitting next to him, hunched over his plate, was his father.

He was older than his father.

And this was his grandmother, and that baby she was carrying was his Aunt Rebecca.

Brann could recognize his father now, in the eyes and the wide mouth, and Kevin's ears were long, too, just like his father's ears were.

Brann swallowed hard: it *had* to be true. And he realized it was something true that he'd been denying to himself since he'd arrived in this place—time.

He was older than his father, and the father he'd just been talking about to his grandfather was the boy sitting next to him; and his grandfather that he'd talked about to Kevin the night before was this strong man who bullied his family but would end up not knowing who he was, never remembering the name of his son Kevin, who was the only one to come visit him, calling Kevin Stevie or Billy, but never by his own name.

Brann was in his father's house, the edge of the chair hard against the backs of his legs, real. He was older than his father, and this was crazier than anything he'd ever imagined.

three

□□□□□□□□□□□□□□□□□□□□□□□□□

BRANN sat at the table while Kevin and his mother cleared the plates, while Kevin's grandmother made up a tray of coffee and pancakes to carry upstairs to his grandfather, and the children ran out of the room into another room where you could hear them quarreling. Kevin helped his mother wash the dishes, Brann noticed, and he thought to himself that he should get up and help his father and grandmother by drying . . .

He couldn't get it straight, that was the trouble. Brann shook his head, to clear it. Of all the impossible, unexpected—but he better be careful. Here, in this house, he was Brann Smith with a family on Second Street, and if he didn't start thinking like Brann Smith he would get himself in trouble.

He stood up and offered to help Mrs. Connell with the dishes. She gave him a towel and passed him a glass to dry. He stood and stared at her. He'd never seen his grandmother. She died when his father was twelve—in

39

two years this woman would die, and that would be 1939, the year Hitler invaded Poland.

"You going to dry or stare?" she demanded.

Brann had to forget about the past that was still the future. "Dry, ma'am, Mrs. Connell."

Her hands were quick in the sink, and between them he and Kevin could barely keep up with her.

"You'll take Suzanne and the rest down to play by the river this morning," Mrs. Connell said to Kevin. "Be back by half past eleven, no later. I'll have lunch waiting."

"Yes, ma'am," Kevin said. He handled the plates carefully, as if he expected himself to drop them. He dried slowly, at half Brann's speed.

"Are you planning to spend the day?" she asked Brann. He said he was if it was all right with her. "Kevin's got responsibilities this morning," she said. "I'm doing the books this afternoon, and checking invoices. Stevie comes with me and the other three go next door, but if anything happens it's all up to Kevin here, when I'm gone. He's the eldest."

"That's OK," Brann said.

She turned to Kevin. "Look in on your grandmother before you go out, to see if they need anything. It's all need and no help, from both of them these days."

"I'll take care of it, Mom."

"You're going to have to."

"When is your baby due?" Brann asked. His Aunt Rebecca, a tiny baby, not even born yet.

"Six weeks, in early August," she said. "It can't be soon enough for me. I need the hospital rest, I'll tell you. From the heat, and the kicking all night long—if this one isn't a boy I'll eat that dishrag."

She swabbed out the sink, scoured it with cleanser, told them to put the dry dishes away, and lumbered out to the living room where the little children were.

"What if it's a girl?" Brann asked Kevin. He tried to keep himself from staring at the boy. His father.

"It won't be. My mom always knows."

TO GET to the river, they had to walk down the street, across a boulevard, down two more blocks and then across railroad tracks. Kevin held Stevie by the hand and the twins ran ahead, waiting by the tracks. They had to stand there while a long freight train went by. Suzanne pitched pieces of cinder at the passing cars. Kevin told her to stop, but not as if he expected her to listen to him. She didn't. What she needed, Brann thought, was a rap on the gums.

Suzanne was tall and skinny, as tall as her older brother, and she had a big, sulky mouth. She looked like the kind of person to whom life is always disappointing. The twins were loud and filled with energy. Stevie, trying to pull his hand free from Kevin's, seemed quiet by comparison, but he glared at Kevin and at Brann, as if he blamed both of them for his hand being held and would get even when he could.

After the train had roared by, the twins and Suzanne ran across. Kevin carried Stevie, who kicked because he didn't want to be picked up, across the two sets of tracks. Brann trailed along.

Another road, dirt this time, and then a broad,

empty lawn, scattered with trees, lay between the railroad tracks and the green river. Off to the right was the house the lawn belonged to, its porches falling down, its second story gaping and charred after a fire.

"Stay on the lawn," Kevin said. The children burst away from him, before he had finished speaking. "I gotta stay at the other end, in case they try to sneak down the bank." Brann could see the river glistening between the trunks of trees.

"Can't they swim?"

"No, except me and Suzanne. Can you?"

"Of course."

Kevin sat down under a cherry tree, old and gnarled, but giving plenty of shade. He faced the lawn where his brothers and sisters were playing. The twins fought over a branch of honeysuckle they both wanted. They yanked on it, each trying to get it away from the other, stripping the leaves off and screaming from anger. Brann stood still, looking around.

He saw the green, neglected grass of the lawn and the many tall trees. He saw the shape of the burned house, as it might have been before the fire. He looked over the green water to the wooded hillsides across the river. "Boy, is it pretty here," he said, thinking of the little square plots of flattened land he'd come from, dotted with rows of shoebox houses, where none of the trees had lived long enough to gain much height.

"It's hot," Kevin answered.

Even at this early hour, the temperature had mounted. The air hung heavy and no wind stirred the many branches.

"It is," Brann agreed, "but not like a city gets hot.

The trees and bushes and even the grass, they cool things down. Why don't you take them wading?"

"In the Ohio River?" Kevin sounded shocked. "My mom would kill me. The river—it's not safe, not even for fish. Grandma says when she was young everybody fished in the river, and swam in it too. But now—you can get sick and die from the stuff in that river. Go look at it and tell me you want to swim in it."

Brann clambered and slid down the steep over-grown bank, grabbing onto saplings when he thought he might fall. The bank went almost straight down for fifteen feet. He had to work to keep his balance. At the bottom, he braced his legs against a fallen tree and looked at the river.

Kevin was right: Pollution was already here. (Brann had thought pollution—in 1974—was a new problem. Things were worse with the world than he'd known.) The water wasn't green from reflecting the hills across the river. It was green with unhealthy algae, and floating on it were stringy brown globs of something Brann was glad he'd never heard the name of. Where the river oozed up to the shore, gray bubbles appeared on islands of debris—branches, pieces of wood, scraps of tire rubber. And it smelled, like garbage and sewage mixed in with the tangy odor of tidal marsh-lands; a faint, unpleasant odor seemed to float along the top of the river.

He scrambled back up the steep slope. "What causes that? Who's responsible?"

Kevin looked up at him without much interest. "The city, I guess, Pittsburgh. The mills and factories. People dump their garbage in."

"Sewage too, I bet," Brann said grimly. "You ought to stop them."

"Stop who? How? You can't do anything. It's too late. Grandma said they used to go out in the winter and cut huge blocks of ice out of it. The people in the big houses up the hill would store the blocks in straw and sawdust, in their spring houses. They'd have ice all summer long. Nobody would want to do that now."

"Ke-ye-vie," Suzanne called down from the top of a tree.

Kevin looked up. "That's too high. Come down." She thumbed her nose at him and leaned out, holding on with just one hand, waving with the other. Kevin turned his back to her and sat down again under the tree.

Brann shrugged and sat in the shade beside Kevin. "Big houses? What big houses? Bigger than yours? Your house is pretty big."

"Not like these. These belong to the rich people, who own the mills and coal mines and things. They're beautiful, there are statues in the gardens and swimming pools, and the houses look—different. I've never been in a swimming pool."

"I have," Brann said, before he thought.

"That isn't true. Is it?"

Brann lied quickly. "There was a kid at my school, his grandmother had one. He invited all the boys over one day and we went swimming and had lemonade."

Kevin believed that. "Once when I was little," he said, "before things got really bad and we had to move in with Grandpa—we used to have our own house, but my father got laid off." Brann nodded. He didn't have to pretend sympathy about fathers who were failures. Except Thomas Connell didn't seem like he was a failure. "We went to a lake once. The twins weren't born. I learned how to swim. I don't remember it much." Brann waited to hear something interesting, but Kevin didn't say anything more. Kevin kept his eyes on the other children.

Stevie stood watching the twins, across the lawn by an overgrown woods. The two dark-haired figures were quarreling about something, stooping over and then pulling one another up and away. They pushed and jerked at one another. It looked like there was something on the ground that they both wanted to keep the other from getting.

Kevin got up slowly and walked over. Brann followed.

"It's mine, Hannah!" Billy yelled. "I caught it!"

"It's the one I found! I remember the hump in its middle!"

Billy jammed his elbow into her stomach. She punched him in the side of the neck.

Two bewildered frogs quivered in the long grass.

"OK, stop now," Kevin said.

"We're racing them!" Hannah yelled into his face, as if that explained everything. Kevin looked helplessly at Brann. Stevie stood behind the twins, sucking one thumb, the other hand behind his back, his eyes watching.

"You ought to leave them alone," Kevin said.

Billy ignored him. "Suzanne?" he whined. "They won't go, they won't even start."

"Prod 'em," Suzanne suggested. She shoved in front of Kevin, a stick in her hand. She jabbed at one of the frogs with it. The frog leaped ahead, then froze again.

"That's mine!" shrieked Hannah.

Stevie brought his hand out from behind his back and threw a stone at the frogs. He missed, but they both jumped in alarm. Then stopped. Stevie trundled off to get more stones.

"Where's the end of the race?" Suzanne asked the twins. They pointed to the honeysuckle vine, laid down twenty feet away. "You could throw things at them," Suzanne suggested. "Or each get a stick. I don't think they're much on racing."

The twins ran off to get sticks. Stevie returned with a handful of stones, which he showered down on the frogs. Suzanne watched the uninteresting results. When his hands were empty, the three-year-old went off for fresh supplies. Suzanne prodded with her bare foot at one of the frogs. It leaped sideways.

It made Brann sick. "Why don't you stop them?" he asked Kevin.

"How? They always do this. They used to take them home and keep them in shoeboxes, but Mom made them stop because the frogs always died and then they stank. What did you say last night? It's fate."

"Fate, my left foot," Brann said. He knew he was angry—and his mother would have known too because she would have seen how his eyes got cold, icy gray. But Kevin didn't know.

The twins ran up, brandishing sticks. Eagerly, they jabbed at the frogs.

"That's it," Brann said, just the way his mother said it. His voice was low and cold. "That's the end of this game. Leave the frogs alone."

"Says who?" Suzanne faced him with a stick in her hand. She was an ugly kid, and if she hadn't been a girl he wouldn't have wasted any words on her, he would have just pasted her one.

"I say," Brann said. He looked at her, feeling the anger shooting out of his eyes. "I don't like torturing frogs."

"Yeah? Well, maybe I do."

"Too bad for you then, isn't it?" Brann stared at her for several minutes. He could see her making up her mind. The twins and Stevie watched, interested in what was going on. Finally, Suzanne threw down her stick—close enough to make the frogs jump, but not exactly at them—and ran off. Brann turned his attention to the twins. "You two, did you hear that?"

"We don't have to do what you say!" Hannah yelled.

"Oh yeah?" Brann asked quietly.

They gave in right away. Only Stevie stood watching Brann, his thumb in his mouth, his blue eyes like somebody looking down a microscope.

Brann turned on his heels and walked back to the old cherry tree. What a family.

Kevin ran up beside him. "That was great! I've told them and told them, and about how the frogs must feel too, but they never did what I said. How'd you do it?" His eyes gleamed with admiration.

Brann didn't know. He just saw that something had to be done and he did it. A train roared by, so he didn't have to answer. He shrugged. After the caboose had rattled off and curved away, he said, "You could, too."

Kevin shook his head. "Anyway," he started, then didn't finish the sentence. "And my mother's going to have another one. Another boy. But I'll be older then, when I have to take care of him, so probably I can manage it better, like you did. Being older helps, doesn't it?"

"I guess so." Being older never was going to help Kevin, Brann thought. He wondered how old Kevin had been when he finally figured that out. "Let's do something."

"What?"

"I don't know. What do you and your friends do around here?"

"I don't have any. Anyway."

"What about the other kids?" Brann was getting impatient. "What do they do?"

"They play baseball, kickball. If they can swim and have a place, they do that. There are some caves, but they're dangerous and we're not supposed to. There are lots of woods around. And stuff, you know."

"Caves? I've never been in caves."

"It's dangerous. They say the caves run all the way under the river because it used to be part of the underground railway, for escaping slaves. Sometimes kids have gotten lost in them. So we're not allowed."

"We could play catch." Brann was getting restless.

"With what?"

"There must be something. A stone? C'mon, Kevin, let's do *something*."

48

They played catch with stones for a while. Another train went by and then another. At that, Kevin dropped the stone and called his brothers and sisters. "And please hurry," he asked them. At that they all slowed down, especially Suzanne, who pretended she had to run back for something. "My mom will have my hide," Kevin said desperately to Brann. Stevie sucked his thumb and looked up at his brother, considering.

Kevin herded them back across the tracks and down the streets. Brann recognized the house now, a sturdy stucco construction that reminded him of Mr. Connell. They ran into the house, Kevin first and Brann after him dragging Stevie by the hand. The twins and Suzanne lagged half a block behind.

The kitchen was bright with midday sunlight, but Mrs. Connell loomed like a dark storm, even sitting down at the table. Her anger filled the whole room, and it rushed to the door to meet Kevin.

She held Kevin responsible. Only Kevin. Brann, slipping into a chair, did what Suzanne did when she sat down: picked up his spoon and started eating. He was more careful to eat quietly than he ever was in his own house. The rest of the children ignored the scene and ate as if nothing was happening. Only Kevin, hunched over his bowl with his hands in his lap, didn't eat.

Mrs. Connell had already finished lunch. Her bowl was pushed away into the center of the table and a half-eaten slab of bread lay on the checkered oilcloth. "Late again."

"I'm sorry," Kevin mumbled.

"Twice a week I ask you to be on time and twice a week you're late."

"I'm sorry. But Mom—"

"I don't want any excuses," she cut him off. "You're the oldest and it's your job, and if it's a whipping you need to do it properly, it's a whipping you'll get." She brushed her dim hair back off her forehead. "It's not much responsibility we ask you to take and you can't even manage that. Can't you get it through your head? We can't afford to hire somebody to do the books and invoices, or to clean the house, or to keep you all in clothes, or make meals."

"I'm sorry," Kevin said again. She didn't listen.

"I can't do everything. You have to help me. You're old enough to take a little responsibility, more than old enough to know how to get back here on time. Instead you go lollygagging around at the river. And what's going to happen when this baby comes, I ask you that. When I'm in the hospital, who's going to take care of things? Your father has to work. Your grandmother— she's close to useless, you know that. I have to count on you. And I can't count on you, can I."

Her voice droned on and on, hammering down on Kevin. Brann thought of speaking up, saying that Suzanne wouldn't come when Kevin told her and the twins followed her when she ran off, but it was Kevin's job to tell that.

As she was talking, and the rest of them were eating, the grandmother shuffled into the room. She ladled soup from the pot on the stove into a tall pitcher and put it onto a tray where two bowls and a plate of bread had been set out. She picked this up and shuffled off, her face vacant. She was pretending she didn't hear.

Kevin sat alone under his mother's anger. He

didn't even pick up his soup spoon. His mother rubbed at her swollen belly with one hand as she hammered and hammered on him.

Poor Kevin. Brann felt a mixture of sympathy for the boy, anger at Suzanne, and frustration that Kevin didn't fight back at all. (And then he'd gone and married a woman who talked to him exactly like this; later when he'd grown up and could have chosen someone else. Why would he do a thing like that?)

"You'll have to wash up by yourself and bring down your grandparents' tray and wash that when they're through. There's fried chicken on the sideboard and nobody's to touch it—it's for your father and Uncle Andrew for supper. Stevie, drink your milk up. The rest of you—put yourselves into your rooms now for naps. I'll phone when it's time to come out." Suzanne and the twins left the table obediently.

Mrs. Connell's eye fell on Brann. "You're not much of a friend," she said to him.

Brann met her eye and his mouth closed on the words he could have said, that he wasn't any friend of Kevin's. Because then he wouldn't have any reason for being there and then—he couldn't begin to think about that. She didn't even know him, how could she pretend to know what kind of friend he was. Besides, keeping the little kids in order was Kevin's job and he wasn't even related to them. (But he was. But that wasn't what he meant.) Besides, she had a pretty unrealistic idea of what it meant to be a friend. Besides, next time Brann would help more. (Next time? What did he mean, next time?)

Mrs. Connell was watching Kevin. Finally the

boy spoke: "I'm sorry." His eyes slid away from hers and he picked up his spoon. He looked like he was trying not to cry. Mrs. Connell spat out an angry breath of air and took Stevie out the back door, a brown paper bag in her other hand.

Brann got up and ran some hot water into the sink. He washed and rinsed the six bowls, then the six glasses, then the six spoons. He dried them and carefully put them away in the cupboards.

Kevin washed his own bowl and spoon, glass, and the bread plate. Brann dried. After a while he asked, "Why *were* we late?"

"I think the trains must have been running late. And I haven't been late but once before, honest."

"Your mother sure has a temper," Brann said. "Suzanne does what she says, though, even going up for a nap."

"We always do, for a couple of hours after lunch in the summer."

"You too?"

"Yeah," Kevin said. His whole face sagged. He looked at Brann and his eyes were gray pools into which Brann could not see.

"What do you do up there?"

"Nothing much. You gonna go now?"

"No," Brann said. He didn't want to stay, but he didn't have any other ideas about what to do. No ideas at all. "At least, if it's OK with you I'll stay."

Kevin's face lit up. "You mean that? I thought— after my Mom—and this morning—and I— It's not very nice here."

Brann shrugged. "It's not as bad as all that."

"Yes, it is," Kevin answered, and Brann couldn't really argue.

THIS TIME, as they walked through the house, Brann looked at the rooms they passed through. There was a dining room with a glass chandelier hanging over the heavy table and a living room where the sofa and chairs all looked fat and soft to sit on. In his own house, the furniture was modern, the rooms were sparsely furnished and they were always filled with light during the day. In this house, the shades were down and a misty light floated through the cluttered rooms.

(His own house wasn't even built yet. If he went to find it, it wouldn't be there. How was he going to find his way back? When he didn't even know how he'd found his way here. His mind ran away from that question.)

They went up a broad staircase, with a wooden banister that gleamed with polish and use. The stairs had carpet on them, worn smooth. The long hallway he'd walked in darkness last night was shorter than he'd thought. Six doors opened onto it. Kevin opened two and looked into the rooms behind.

Suzanne and Hannah shared a bedroom. Hannah was asleep, but Suzanne was sitting on her bed playing with a teddy bear. She hid it behind her when she saw the boys.

"Hey, Brann, you look like you've got some guts, you wanna come swimming with me?"

"In that river? Not on your life."

"Not in the river—I'm not stupid. I know a house that's empty. They went away somewhere for the summer. They left the pool full. It's risky, you could get caught, but the pool's just waiting to be swum in. What do you say? Kevin never will—he's a sissy."

Brann looked coolly at her. "I might," he said. He waited for her victorious smile to get settled on her face before he added, "and I might not."

Billy had a big room all to himself. He was sitting at the window. "I'm here so get out," was all he said.

"Stevie will sleep in with Billy when the new baby comes," Kevin explained to Brann as they went down the hall. "That's my parents' room and that's Stevie's. There's a guest room." They climbed up the dark attic stairs.

"How come you're upstairs, not with the rest of them?" Brann asked.

"So I can keep an eye on my grandparents," Kevin explained. "In case something happens, or they need something."

"Because you're the oldest."

The two old people sat in a small living room across from their bedroom, at the end of the hallway. A fan pulled warm air through the low-ceilinged room and out the one window. The man was looking at a magazine, his face expressionless. The woman was piling their lunch dishes onto the tray. "It's ready, Kevin," she said, in her airy voice. "Hello. Are you a friend of Kevin's?"

Brann hesitated. He had already met her at breakfast, but maybe she had forgotten.

"It's Brann, Brann with two n's," Kevin said, with a smile to take any criticism out of his words. "You met him at breakfast, but you forgot. I'll take the tray down, Grandma." He picked it up and left the room. Brann was left standing.

"It's good for Kevin to have a friend over," the woman said to Brann. "He doesn't have enough friends. Did you meet him at school? Kevin's going into the fifth grade next fall. I had a teacher in fifth grade—long division, Miss Mead. That was my last year at school." She tilted her head and looked up at Brann through her washed-out eyes. "I surprised you, didn't I? But it was —we left school earlier in those days, but you wouldn't remember that. Do you remember Miss Mead?"

"No ma'am," Brann said.

"She always wore a sprig of something pinned on the collar of her blouse. In the fall it would be a mum or a maple leaf. In winter, holly or a bit of pine. But in spring, you never knew what it would be, daisies or crocuses, roses, jonquils, hyacinth, quince or cherry blossoms. . . . She wasn't happy—surely you recall that. No young man would want to marry the schoolteacher, of course. She went away, or so I heard. I don't know for sure—I'd left years before. When will you leave school?"

"After college, I guess," Brann said, without thinking.

But that was all right. She wasn't listening to him. Her mind was far away. Brann edged towards the door. Kevin came back into the room and stood beside Brann.

"It was always oatmeal for breakfast, all my life," his grandmother complained.

"You had pancakes this morning, Grandma."

"Don't talk about this morning—this morning doesn't count. It was always oatmeal. Thick, pale, pasty. *Stick to your ribs*, she'd say. I could have thrown it up."

"Anyway," Kevin said.

"What do you know about it? What did I know then? I was your age once, just you remember that. All the oatmeal days. All the oatmeal people. Not you, Kevin."

Kevin shook his head. "Yes, I am."

"You're oatmeal with honey then, or crumbled maple sugar that coats the top and melts down the hills of it. But it won't make any difference. I'm sorry, Kevin." Her hands rubbed nervously against one another.

"I'll tell you what," Kevin said. "Shall I make your breakfast tomorrow and bring it up on a tray? Scrambled eggs, the way you like them. And toast with the crusts cut off and raspberry jam to put on it."

"I wouldn't want the jam," she said, quieter.

"The coffee in your best china cup, from the cupboard in the dining room. And on the tray—I'll put a lace doily and I'll get a rose in a vase; a rose that's just coming into bloom so it'll last for days. I'll make the tray and I'll carry it upstairs and I'll knock on the door."

"They won't let you."

"We can pretend. Can't we? Brann's got to go now." He signaled Brann with his eyes. Grateful, Brann sidled out of the room.

"Who's Brann?" her voice asked, getting high again. "Should I know him? Do I have a grandchild Brann?"

"Brann's nobody, you don't know him."

"I didn't think so." The voices follcwed Brann down the hall.

Kevin's room was as he remembered it, with one window and the bed up against the rest of that wall. Blocks lay scattered around on the floor. Brann closed the door behind him and crouched down to pick up the mess he'd made last night, waking up.

What was he going to do?

How was he going to get out of here?

He began stacking the blocks into piles, to avoid thinking.

On the back of the door, a picture had been taped to the wood. It showed a farmyard and some hills beyond and an orchard. It was pretty crude and childish, done in pencil then crayoned in; but the house and barn looked solid, as if they were really there. The lines of the house and barn were strong, and the perspective was right. Brann's father had taught him about perspective. There were some animals in the picture. Brann's attention was caught by the chickens who scrabbled around for the feed being thrown to them by a stick-figure woman. Those chickens were good, really good. They looked alive, as if in a minute they would start moving around. Brann stood studying the picture, holding one of the curved blocks in his hand. The block felt familiar, and that comforted him. It should feel familiar, he thought; they were his same blocks, just paler than he was used to, light white-yellow. He rubbed his hands over the block, knowing that the oil from his skin was sinking invisibly into the warm wood. He could almost see the dark workroom and the shape of his father's worktable and himself, asleep in the fortress his father had built out of these same blocks.

Kevin jarred him out of his dream, opening the door and entering the room. But Brann had figured it out. It was simple after all. It was impossible, but simple. It was the blocks. They had brought him here and they would take him back. So he wasn't trapped in the past. He could get out whenever he wanted, and he knew how.

Relief made him giddy. It was all impossible, of course. Blocks couldn't do that. But he *was* here, in this *now* that wasn't his own.

He dropped the block. Kevin's face, looking at the farmyard picture, came into sharp focus. Brann grinned and put a hand on Kevin's shoulder. He could feel happiness spreading out from him. "You drew that, didn't you?"

"Yeah."

"I like the chickens—they're really good."

Kevin studied it. "You think so? I thought so too. But there's an awful lot wrong with it. The barn is always in the shadow of that big elm—see it? I drew it from memory, but I didn't get much right."

"What is it?" Brann asked, although he had already guessed, and he knew he was right—his brain was swinging fast and sharp.

"My Uncle Andrew's farm. Where I go every summer, to work, and to get out from underfoot. I like that place." His eyes were dreaming into the picture.

"Why?" Brann asked. "I mean, farming's really hard work, isn't it?"

"I guess," Kevin said. "But it's—I don't know. You're working and you're tired, all day long, but— Uncle Andrew's funny, he makes me laugh. He talks, all the time, but not about what to do next, about what life is like, sort of. It sounds stupid. But it's interesting, and I have ideas there, pictures and things. It's an easy place to live. He's my godfather, anyway. He married my mother's sister and he made me these blocks when I was four. He worked on them all one winter."

Kevin sat down among the blocks. Slowly, placing each block thoughtfully, he began to build a tower with them, and connected it by arches to a series of small outbuildings. Brann watched.

"I'm gonna have to give them to Billy soon," Kevin said. "He doesn't take care of things, but my father says I'm too old for blocks now and Billy's old enough. Then Stevie will be. I wish I didn't have to."

"You can get them back in the end," Brann said.

"Then this new baby boy—"

"It could be a girl."

Kevin shook his head. "Mom says it's a boy."

"Anyway, you can get them back when everybody else has outgrown them. For your own kids."

Kevin shook his head again. "I don't think so.

"People grow up and marry people," Brann told him impatiently. "And they have kids."

"I'd only want a small family."

"I have a small family," Brann said.

"Only one or two."

"What about three?" Brann asked.

"I don't think so," Kevin said.

"Can I build a wall along here?" Brann asked.

"Could you build it over there?" Kevin pointed to a line of floorboard six inches farther away. "It'll look better. More as if it was real. You don't mind playing with blocks?"

"Not a bit," Brann said. "Not these blocks." His relief had turned into a feeling of secret celebration, that danced inside of him. Because he was the one, Brann Connell, who had done this, gone back in time; that made him pretty special, special and terrific. There must be some special reason that got him back here.

Kevin was looking at him, smiling shyly. He was such a little kid, Brann thought, and not much of a little kid at that. About the opposite of special. "Are you my friend?" Kevin asked, with the same hesitating smile, his eyes slipping away. "No," he said, right away before Brann could think of an answer, "That was stupid. Forget I said it, OK? I mean, I know you'll be moving on and all that."

"I've got to," Brann answered. Now I know how, he thought to himself. Besides, he'd go crazy living in this house. He wondered why Kevin hadn't gone crazy already. "I really have to," he said. "It's fate."

That was what you said when you couldn't possibly explain.

four

□□□□□□□□□□□□□□□□□□□□□□□□□□□□

THE two boys had finished the castle close. That was Kevin's name for it. Brann would have named it a fortress. It was a castle enclosed by a tall wall, like a fence around a farmyard. The boys made little buildings inside the wall, sheds and storage barns, for animals and for supplies; an overseer's house, a blacksmith's forge, a silversmith's hut, a mill and a granary, a gardener's hut (because the castle itself had extensive vegetable gardens). Kevin explained that the serfs would have had their homes outside the close, near the fields. The gateway, built up as high as Brann's knees, was broad enough to let to wagons through. It would have had a heavy spiked gate that was lowered every evening and raised in the morning. If the lord was away from his castle, the gate would always be kept down and only raised to admit people who were recognized by the lady or the steward. But if the lord was home then the castle gate was kept raised during the day, because he could fight to defend it.

"What if he was too old to fight?" Brann asked. "What if he was a bad fighter, or a coward?"

"He wouldn't have the castle if he couldn't fight to hold it. He'd have lost it to some other lord and he might go be a monk and illustrate manuscripts, or be in service to some stronger lord. If he was old—like my grandfather, you mean? He'd have his sons, and the eldest son would run things and the lord would move into a tower or someplace out of the way."

"How do you know all this?"

"I read a book," Kevin said. "My grandparents didn't have any sons, only daughters."

"It's hot up here," Brann said. With the door closed, the one window didn't draw any air in. Brann's whole body felt sticky with sweat. He went to stand by the window, looking down at the yard and the roof of the garage and the big house behind this one.

"Because it's a river valley—the Ohio River Valley —and the air goes along the river. It's always hot and muggy here in summer."

"And the caves go right under the river? Like a tunnel?" Brann asked.

"That's what they say. But not like a tunnel. Because they're caves formed when rocks shift, or slide, the strata, you know? Not by erosion like caverns."

"I wouldn't mind seeing those caves. Have you ever been in them?"

Kevin shook his head. Of course not, Brann thought, looking at him; he'd be too scared.

"What's that farm like?" Brann asked, just to be

doing *something*, even just talking. Kevin told him about the hills and the river there, the same river, the Ohio, only dirtier because of the big mill towns along it, between Sewickley and the farm. Kevin talked about harvesting hay, about milking cows so early in the morning that stars still shone in the sky, and about mucking out the stalls and the mingled smells of manure and dry hay and warm animals. He talked about spending all morning on a tractor, to weed out the long rows of corn, and the way the sun beat down until the skin on your hands cracked, and you had to hold the wheel so hard—because if you didn't the sweat would make it slip out of control and you'd rip out the young corn plants—that you could barely unclench your hands at the end of the day. His Uncle Andrew talked all the time, stories and advice about life, jokes.

"You really like your uncle, don't you?" Brann asked. He wondered why his father had never talked about Uncle Andrew.

"Yeah. I guess I do. And he likes me," Kevin answered. "He really does."

"Are you going to be a farmer when you grow up?" Brann expected the answer to be yes.

"I don't know what I'm going to be. I'd like to draw—magazines have a lot of drawings in them and someone must do them. Or greeting cards and calendars. My mother says that's all well and good, but I should be practical. She says I should look for something that uses drawing, because otherwise I won't be able to earn a living."

"Does she like your drawings?"

"She likes them OK," Kevin said. "She says, I'm

no genius but I have some talent, and you have to work on talent to train it."

Brann nodded. That was good advice, even if it didn't sound exactly enthusiastic.

"She wouldn't say that if she didn't mean it," Kevin announced, with confidence.

"I guess not," Brann said. "Why didn't you tell her it was Suzanne's fault this morning?"

Kevin shrugged. "Anyway, it was my responsibility."

"When can we go out again?" Brann asked. He was getting really restless, with this feeling . . . exploding inside him, waiting to find out what the special thing would be.

"When my mother calls."

"Show me some drawings, will you?"

When the phone rang three times, then stopped, the two boys were sitting on the bed, looking at some drawings Kevin had made of faces. (He didn't know how to make noses. He drew a nose in one line and then put two nostril dots beside it. Brann's father had taught him how to make noses by shading.) Kevin took the three little children down the street to stay with a neighbor. "They go there two afternoons a week, when my mom does the books," he explained to Brann. "The Grynowskis have six kids of their own, and she feeds them supper. Other days their kids come to our house."

"I'm glad I came on a day when yours are going there," Brann said. Suzanne stuck her tongue out at him. Brann decided to wait for Kevin on the back steps.

"You won't go away, will you?" Kevin asked. "I'll

only be five minutes, maybe ten. Then we can do something."

Brann couldn't possibly fall asleep in five or ten minutes. He wasn't even tired. All of his nerves were jangling. "I'll be here," he said, He felt trapped, even though he knew the way to get out, even though he was waiting for his adventure to begin. Every hour in this place—time—was like a year, a heavy and hopeless year. And thinking about Kevin—about his father—who lived there—it made Brann feel even more jangled. He really wanted to go back home—except he was curious to know why this was happening for him.

Kevin was running when he came back. He stopped in front of where Brann sat on the porch steps. "What do you want to do?" he asked.

"I want to see those caves."

"Why?"

"I've never seen caves."

"I'm sorry," Kevin said. "We can't. We're not allowed."

"But who would know? Is it far?"

"No, but—"

"Have you got a flashlight?"

"Yes, but—"

"Let's get it."

Brann had made up his mind and he just swept Kevin along, because the kid was easy to sweep along. The way to do it was just not to give him time to answer. The flashlight was in a kitchen drawer, a heavy metal one, and Kevin ran upstairs to tell his grandparents he was going out now.

"We aren't allowed," Kevin reminded Brann.

"You aren't allowed," Brann told him. "Nobody's said anything to me." That was a weak argument, he knew, but he also knew how to win arguments with Kevin, like his mother did. "Look, I know you're scared but you don't have to go in or anything. I just want to see them. You won't be breaking any rules or anything. You aren't scared just to take me there, are you?"

Kevin shook his head, no, his face ashamed.

"Then let's go," Brann urged him.

They crossed a couple of streets, then went up a road that wound with steep curves up a wooded hillside. They trudged up the hillside, with Brann urging Kevin to go faster, to keep going. "I'm sorry," Kevin said. Brann didn't answer, just grunted his impatience.

Along the top of the hill was a cemetery, with dirt roads twisting through it. The entrance to the cemetery was marked by a statue of an angel with a sword, a monument to the men who died in the Civil War. Brann turned to look down the steep wooded hillside. At the foot of the hill the houses of the town began. Beyond, he saw the Ohio River, lying in the sun. It didn't look bad from that distance, especially with the wooded hills rising on its far side.

"It's nice, isn't it?" Kevin asked.

It was cooler up on the hill. All around thick green grass spread between the tombstones, and lush trees spread their branches. But nice?

"There's nothing nice about being dead," Brann said. "Let's go."

This steep, blufflike hill undulated back into grassy fields, with woods edging them. The entrance to the caves was right at the edge of a field, where a few trees grew. A sudden short hillside among the sparse trees lay covered with dried leaves from past falls and a few dead branches. The opposite hillside rose up as sharply, making a miniature ravine. Kevin led Brann halfway down the slope, the leaves rustling under their bare feet, making it sound like fall underfoot even though the air around them was thick with summer. "They're here," Kevin said.

Brann looked around. "Here?" He looked for some undergrowth that would mask the entrance to a cave.

The entrance wasn't masked, it was just hard to see. It didn't look like the entrance to anything. It looked like the narrow end of the ravine, with the big tree roots above. But once you knew where to look, you could see through the natural camouflage to a narrow slipping away, where a gap was created by the floor of the ravine falling down below the rise of the hill. Brann went right up to the entrance. It was so low, he had to bend over to shine the flashlight in. Kevin stood ten feet behind him, and even with his back to the younger boy Brann could feel the fear pouring out of him. He didn't pay any attention.

The beam of light showed the floor falling away. It looked like a slide, you could slide right down it.

"I've never been in a cave," Brann said, without moving his head.

"Anyway," Kevin answered.

"I'm going in," Brann decided.

"Don't. Please?"

"Look, other kids must have, if they talk about it. That's true, isn't it?"

"Yes, but—"

"I won't go far. You don't have to come." In fact, Brann didn't want Kevin with him. This was his adventure, for him. "Wait here, I won't be long."

"But Brann—"

Brann lay on his back, his legs extending into the sloped entrance. He held the flashlight against his abdomen, to protect it with his body in case the tunnel narrowed unexpectedly. He elbowed himself forward and down.

"Brann?" he heard behind him, before he slid out of hearing.

The leaves hadn't entered far into the tunnel, and he could move under his own control, he could even sit up, resting his torso on his elbows. He could have walked down hunched over, he realized, it wasn't so steep after all, and the roof was higher than he'd thought. Daylight filtered in behind him and the beam of the flashlight probed ahead.

The slope lasted no more than twenty feet. At its end the floor leveled and Brann sat for a minute, moving the flashlight around. It was about the size of a walk-in closet, this area. A couple of spider webs, but everything else rocks: uneven rock walls, an uneven rock floor, the ceiling smoother rock. There was still a little daylight behind him.

Brann stood up and examined the walls. If it was part of the underground railway, there had to be a way forward, unless that was just a story. But Kevin didn't tell stories like that, to boast. He moved around to the right, along the wall, and sure enough he saw a narrow opening, behind an outcrop of rock. It was half his height, and he crouched down to send the flashlight beam in. A kind of tunnel; he'd have to crawl. But at the end, deeper darkness, like another room, and not a long tunnel. Brann made himself look around at the closet room he was in, memorizing the appearance of the outcropping rock. He wasn't going to be careless about this, and he knew he had a good memory. Then he crawled into the tunnel.

No daylight here, nothing but heavy black darkness. The flashlight, held in his right hand, clunked on the ground. Stupid, he said to himself, and moved it to his mouth, thinking that that must be why miners had lights on their hats. He wouldn't like to lose that flashlight or have it break on him.

The stones rubbed at his shoulders and cut sharp at the fabric of his jeans. Like a dog following a scent, he followed the beam of light, slowly, his head down to keep from banging it against the ceiling.

The light splayed out in front of him at the same time he felt the ceiling lift. He felt down, over the edge of the tunnel, with his right hand. Nothing.

Brann felt a second of panic, as pleasurable as a good horror movie. All he had to do was back out the slow ten feet, no problem. No reason to give up. He took the flashlight out of his mouth and shone it ahead. He couldn't see anything across, so it had to be a big room, a real cave. Flat on his belly now, he scraped forward, until his head and shoulders were out in the empty blackness. He directed the light down. And it was going to be easy, he just hadn't reached down far enough to find the floor of this room. It wasn't even a two foot drop, he just had to be careful with the flashlight.

Careful also to memorize what he could. He looked at the shape of the opening, hunching backwards to do so. He hunched forward again and twisted his neck around to check the walls he could see. Then he slowly, cautiously, careful never to come even close to being off balance, edged his body onto the floor of the room. And stood up.

A sharp pain in his heel, a reflex jerk away, but his grip tightened on the flashlight. He'd stepped on something sharp. The light showed uneven stones, some of them sharp edged, jutting up. He should have shoes on. He grinned.

So far so good. Now the misty edge of light showed the shadowy opposite of the room, showed a ceiling five feet over his head. If he stuck to the wall he could check the way the cave went from here. But first he buried the front of the flashlight against his backside, to get the feeling of what it was like in here. He didn't want to turn it off, just in case, but he did want to get the real feeling.

Without light the room moved out around him again, but the dark got heavier, as if the earth above was pressing down on it. It was cool here, and dry. Brann gulped in air, suddenly worried that the air would run out, then reminded himself that he'd have to be a lot deeper, and sealed in somehow, before that could even begin to happen. But it felt like it could happen, with the light gone. It felt like it was happening.

His eyes tried to make out any shape, any shadow, but they couldn't see anything. He felt the dark air closing around his body. He could feel the hard, uneven rock against the soles of his feet. He could hear—nothing, nothing but deep, muffled darkness. He knew you couldn't actually hear nothing, but the hollow sound-lessness was so different from anything he had ever used his ears to hear, it really felt like hearing something. Then he thought he could hear his heart beating fast in his ears. It really was scary. Brann resisted the impulse to free the light for another minute, to let the scariness soak in a little more. If you were lost in a cave, he thought to himself, saying the words out slowly, this is what it would feel like, the earth pressing in all around you, only a narrow belt of air holding it off. And what if there was an earthquake, right now? It wouldn't have to be an earthquake. Because of the way strata of rocks were connected underground, once one little thing shifted, rocks for hundreds of miles around would shift too, readjusting. Then the dark walls here would shift, grinding probably, closing off—

He freed the light and shone it around, grinning to himself. He started on his circuit around the room, moving always to the right, knowing that it closed off in basically a circular shape, so as long as he didn't move out of the circle he wouldn't get lost. By looking carefully, he could see occasional entrances off the room, but you had to really use the light to find them, looking beyond and behind the rocks, up and down the walls of the room. He counted three, then up to seven, and then another three.

A lot of entrances for a space that wasn't in fact that big. The caves must spread out like a honeycomb network, like—what did they call the burial places in Rome—the catacombs? You'd really have to know your way around to move out of this room. A couple of the entrances were overhead, unreachable. A couple were like the one he'd used, ledges, and they were the hardest to pick out.

If you were a slave, escaping, you might use one of the entrances that came high up. You would fall down, into darkness. What an idea. And what would it have been like under the river, really deep down, probably with the rock slippery underfoot and the walls slimy, cold all year round, wet, and wondering if the river would make its way through and smash you against the rocks even though you were only an arm's length away from the walls—Brann shivered.

OK, that was enough, it was about time to get back to where Kevin waited. He moved to the right, along the wall, looking for the ledge. He came to it. He didn't realize until he'd found it that he had, in fact, been afraid he wouldn't find it. He put his arm into it and shone the light down it. The beam, narrowed by the low ceiling, reflected off stone and shone back on itself, down an endless tunnel.

Brann's chest tightened, like an iron band had been drawn around it. He put his face into the opening. It wasn't an endless tunnel, he saw; it was a false tunnel, the roof gradually sliding down to meet the floor.

Don't panic, he muttered aloud. Slowly, move on, keep checking. He forced his memory to recreate the shape of the opening he was looking for and forced his muscles to keep slow.

And he couldn't find it.

He tried to remember just how many openings into the room there had been, but then he remembered that probably like a man lost in the woods he had been going in circles and circles, getting nowhere, without any sense of direction—

"Stop it," he told himself. His voice echoed strangely. He had always moved to the right, there was nothing to do with direction in here. It was just recognition. But his memory was crowded with undistinguishable shapes, all of them black and rocky—he couldn't recognize anything.

And the light was getting yellower, and that meant it was giving out, and he'd better find his opening, fast.

Brann's heart beat and his legs shook, partly with the effort required not to break into a run. His hands shook with fear. He gulped for air.

He made himself sit down, crouching with his knees up against his chest, his back against the rough wall. He counted to ten, then twenty. He said the alphabet backwards. He shone the light on his feet, to keep from seeing the stone underground room around him, just a few short feet, really, from the earth's surface—if only he could find it.

He had a couple of cuts on the heel of his right foot. He licked his fingers and wiped the blood off, then licked the blood off his own fingers.

His mind raced around the room, banging up against the walls, trying to remember something, anything that would help. His body wanted to move the same way. What was he going to do? He had to do something; you couldn't just sit there and wait.

Because he was trapped—trapped in this circular cave and he'd be really stupid to try any tunnel he wasn't sure of, because he could crawl deeper away until he died. Of hunger. Of exhaustion. And he'd thought there was some terrific special reason for him to have traveled back in time. Well, maybe this was it, and maybe later a later Brann would come and find his bones. . . . Except that couldn't be, because he was the later Brann. So he was trapped in a time circle, and he'd never even be able to warn that later Brann because he'd never get out, and the later Brann would never know until now, when he was trapped in the cave. That was fate with a vengeance.

Brann sat shaking, his teeth chattering, his unseeing eyes fixed on his ten toes coming out from his feet in two tidy rows. He felt like his brain was cracking in half. He had never thought about how you could go crazy from being afraid. He'd heard of it, of course, but those were just ghost stories. But he had to stop thinking or he would go crazy, he had to stop being afraid, or being this much afraid. But he couldn't.

All right, he said to himself, his chest so tight he had to push it out every time he wanted to take a breath, so what. It's fate. And you had to grab fate if you were worth anything. That's the hard truth, he said to himself, you hear? If you have to grab fate then you grab it, like Arthur grabbed Excalibur to take the sword out of the stone. Because he must have grabbed Excalibur the same way, at the end, to throw it back into the water, the hilt hard and heavy in his hand, and both of them were fate.

The band around Brann's chest tightened and he started to cry—sniveling like a baby, whimpering, he thought in a back corner of his brain. And he couldn't stop, because after all he couldn't grab onto his fate.

He pulled up his T-shirt to wipe his nose on, furious at himself.

"Oh God, what am I going to do?" he wondered, and heard his own terrified voice.

Another voice called his name: "Brann? Brann?"

Stupid chicken, Brann said to himself, sucking in air to clear his nose, rubbing the back of his left hand across his eyes to hide the marks of tears. If he'd only thought, Kevin was outside and he wasn't very far in—he'd panicked. He felt like a jerk, a real jerk. He hoped nothing showed.

"In here," he said. "Can you see the light?"

"Brann?"

"Here," Brann said. He moved out to the center of the room so the light would shine as widely as possible. He turned toward the direction of the sound of a body scraping down a tunnel.

"Brann?"

"See the light?"

"Yes, OK."

Brann shone the light toward the voice. But the echoes had deceived him and Kevin hurried toward him from the darkness behind him. Tripped, stumbled against him, and almost knocked the flashlight out of his hand. Brann wheeled around to shine it in the boy's face.

"I'm sorry," Kevin said.

"No harm done," Brann said, just glad to not be alone in there, glad to see another face. He put his hand on Kevin's shoulders, and relief made his knees weak. The narrow bones under his hand surprised him, they

75

were so round and small. "Let's get going," he said. "I'll tell you—" but he didn't finish the sentence.

Kevin stood aside, waiting for Brann to move. Brann waited for Kevin to move. They looked at one another, in their pale circle of light.

"You didn't mark where you came in?" Brann asked.

"I was worried about you—it was a long time. I'm sorry. Don't you know how to get out?"

"If I did I'd have been out long ago," Brann snapped.

"I'm sorry."

"What are we going to do?" Brann asked, after a long time. "I couldn't find it. I looked and looked and I could only find the wrong ones."

Kevin didn't say anything.

"You should have marked where you came in. You should always do that, it's just common sense," Brann told the boy.

"I'm sorry," Kevin said.

Brann let out an angry breath of air—and heard himself do that, just like his mother did, and his grandmother too. He heard the way he had just been talking to the kid, hammering. His brain had split, he thought to himself, and new things were getting into it.

"No, I should have marked it too and I didn't," he said. "Let's sit down." Why had Kevin followed him in? As long as Kevin was outside to go for help, Brann was OK, he'd finally figured that out. For all the good that did now. Back to the beginning, that's where they'd got to. Trapped still, only Kevin didn't have to worry because it was for sure that Kevin would get out. Maybe that was what Brann's fate was supposed to be, they'd sit and starve and he'd die first and Kevin would chew on his bones and that would save Kevin's life until he was rescued. Then Kevin would grow up and get married and have three children until one disappeared one day.

"Will we die?" Kevin asked him.

"It's no good asking that question," Brann told him.

They sat shoulder to shoulder, and Brann played the flashlight around on the indecipherable walls of stone, not expecting to see anything.

"I guess we could, even so close to the surface. We could, couldn't we. I'd rather die with someone I like, wouldn't you?"

Brann didn't answer. He was staring at Kevin. "Aren't you scared?"

"Sure," Kevin said. "But if you think about it—I mean if it has to happen, if it's fate—I'd much rather with you than anyone else."

Brann couldn't think of what to say. Either the kid was really stupid or he was incredibly brave.

"I mean, I don't know about you, about your family, but if you've run away—and my family, well, they wouldn't care much. Do you think?"

"No," Brann admitted. He was astounded by this kid. "Your mother would."

"She might if she wasn't so busy, but she's too tired and busy. It's not her fault, she just has to be. So it would be OK. I mean"—Kevin smiled his odd, sad smile—"It's not OK at all, but I wouldn't mind that much. What about you, though?"

Where did the kid get that kind of courage? Brann was wondering. "I'm glad you're here, anyway," he said. "I was getting hysterical."

"I don't think so," Kevin told him.

"Oh yeah? Crying like a baby. Cross my heart." Brann crossed his heart.

"I'm sorry," Kevin said.

"Oh Kevin," Brann said. "Look, it's not your fault at all, it's my fault. You warned me." He felt the boy's slight body beside him. "I feel terrible about this." Boy was that inadequate. "I wish my father was here," Brann said without thinking. Without even thinking why he would wish that even under ordinary circumstances.

"My mom says wishes aren't good for anything. She says if wishes were horses beggars would ride."

"Yeah," Brann agreed. Then it struck him—his father *was* here, and that struck him as pretty funny. He began to laugh. "Well, maybe your mother doesn't know everything," he sputtered out, before he began to laugh again.

The laughter restored some of the pride he'd lost, alone. Because if you could laugh then you weren't entirely beaten down. The laughing, while Kevin stared at him as if he was crazy, washed away some of the shame. "Anyway," he said.

"What's your father like?" Kevin asked him. Brann was seized by another fit of laughter. He had to wait to catch his breath to answer.

"He's nothing special, really. He's a nice guy, not successful, nothing special. Except—"

"Yeah?"

"Except, down deep, he's got a way of telling the truth. And that makes him pretty special. I mean, take most people, take me; if I can make people think what I want to have be true about me, then I'm satisfied—whether it's really true or not."

"I don't believe that," Kevin said.

"But not him." Brann grinned to himself, deciding whether or not to say the next thing he thought of. He decided he would: "He's a lot like you."

"Oh," Kevin said. Then, "I'm sorry."

"I'm not," Brann answered, surprising himself. "But we've got this problem, we better get moving."

"Moving?"

Brann answered sarcastically, "You want to sit here and die quietly?"

"I didn't mean that," Kevin apologized. "It's just —when you make something, you have to make it piece by piece and slowly. Putting it together from the bottom up. Maybe I didn't understand what you meant by moving."

But he had, Brann realized. And he was right, because he wasn't scared like Brann was. "OK," he said. Then a question struck him, "Like with people too, relationships get made piece by piece, don't they, that's the way to make relationships."

Kevin shook his head. "Your relatives are born with you, you don't get to do anything. I mean if we try to think about it first, about how we're going to find the way out."

Kevin didn't understand, but Brann did. Maybe

just because he was older. Or maybe because he'd just let his brain split apart so he could let some new ideas in. "We could do a circuit of the walls," he suggested.

"But you already tried that, didn't you?"

"I guess so. And—everything I memorized I forgot as soon as I panicked. I thought I was being so smart. I didn't mean to get you into this kind of trouble, Kevin."

"I know. It's OK, really."

"Can you remember anything?"

"I just followed your voice, until I could see the light, and where you were—you were like a silhouette, because you were shining it in the other direction. The echoes must have confused you, do you think?"

"I don't think, I know. But listen, can you picture it? People who draw, artists—"

"I'm not an artist," Kevin interrupted.

"Yeah, but you must have a good visual memory. Don't argue with me, I'm having an idea, it can't hurt if I just have it. Can you remember where I was standing?"

Kevin thought. Brann waited. While he waited he moved the light beam around the walls. "There," Kevin said.

"Are you sure?"

"Well, there was the shadow from a rock like a huge spear, and I remember that and that rock looks like it might cast that kind of shadow."

Brann got up to stand about as far from the wall as he thought he'd been. Kevin stayed behind him, directing him where to stand until it looked right. "Now," Brann said. "Back off to where you might have come in."

"But I can't see barely anything."

"We need to get a fix on the general area where you came in," Brann explained patiently. "Until it looks, as much as you can remember, just like it did."

"Do I have to?"

"It's the best way to try, I think. If you get too scared I can turn around and shine the light, but if you could just try it—I've been all around these walls seven times and I couldn't see anything and I'm not sure even this will work. So if we can make it as close to how it was, that'll be our best bet. Because your visual memory is what we're banking on."

He heard the shuffling footsteps behind him. It took a long time, until Kevin finally said, "Here."

Brann turned around, shone the light in the direction of Kevin's voice and crossed the room. "There's a ledge," he said, his heart rising, "so far so good." He put the flashlight into the narrow opening.

The beam shone down an endless tunnel, reflecting back upon itself. Brann's heart sank. Now he could see how the roof of the tunnel gradually sank down to meet the floor, closing it off. He drew his arm out of the opening.

"I already tried that one, that's not it." His voice sounded hollow.

"You mean you went in it?"

"No, I looked down it, because it felt like about the

right height. But it's too long, see?" He stepped back to let Kevin look. "It wasn't that long a tunnel and this one just closes down, narrows down. See?"

Kevin peered in. "I don't think so," he said. "It's an optical illusion, because the tunnel slanted down, remember?"

Brann didn't remember that. But he knew he couldn't trust himself. "Shall we try? How long was it, do you remember?"

"Awfully long."

"But you were moving in the dark so that might make it seem longer. I don't know. Why did you come down anyway?"

"I thought maybe you'd hurt yourself or something. You'd been gone a long time."

"You're really something, kid, you know that?"

"No, I'm not. Do you want to try this?"

"We can always back out again. I guess. Let's take a chance on your visual memory."

"I don't know—"

"It's OK," Brann reassured him. "Do you want to go first, or me? We should hold onto ankles or something. So we don't get separated."

"You go first, please," Kevin said.

They clambered into the narrow tunnel. Brann, flashlight in his mouth again, his pace impaired by Kevin's hand holding onto his left ankle, tried to remember how narrow it had seemed before, whether his shoulders had rubbed in the same way, how low he'd had to hold his head, whether it had taken this long, seemed this long a stretch . . .

When he saw the darkness open up ahead, and dim

daylight filtering through with false brightness from overhead, he opened his mouth to tell Kevin. The flashlight clattered on the stones and went out. "It's OK," Brann said, "you were right, we're out!" He scrabbled along the stone floor until he picked up the flashlight. Then he pulled his body out of the tunnel and reached a hand to haul Kevin out. He hugged the boy in sheer relief, feeling how short he was and how narrow his chest. "You did it," he said again.

Kevin nodded, his face pale.

Brann shook the flashlight and it came on again, the batteries rattling inside of the metal tube. "Let's get out of here."

They clambered on all fours up the steep incline, until the earth broke apart over their heads. Above—Brann scrambled up and out—over his head, miles and miles of empty sky—opened out—to pour down light so bright it hurt, and nothing had ever hurt so wonderfully in his whole life.

Kevin was standing in the same dazed fashion. His clothes were covered with dirt, his face was streaked with it, his hair matted down with it. The two boys stared at each other for a minute, then they both broke into a run, to stumble laughing back up out of the trees, to run at full speed across the field. Brann waited for Kevin to catch up at the road, and they made the rest of the journey back at a more sedate pace.

five

WHEN they turned the corner onto Kevin's Street, Kevin stopped Brann. "Don't tell," he said.

"Why not?"

"I'd get in real trouble. Promise?"

"Sure, I promise."

"Never? Promise you'll never tell no matter what?"

Brann thought it was pretty silly, a little kid promise. But it was the least he could do for Kevin who had gotten him out. "I promise, I'll never tell. Not anyone."

Kevin nodded. They started to walk down the sidewalk. "Let me go in and check on my grandparents, then we can get washed up before anybody knows."

"That'll feel good," Brann agreed. Dirt and sweat, heat sweat and fear sweat, both, felt scummy all over his body. He could do with a shower. He sat down on the back steps to wait for Kevin to give him the OK and to think. He wanted to think back over the things he'd been thinking in the cave, when he was scared he'd never get out—and about Kevin. He wanted to let the ideas soak in clearly, so he wouldn't forget them. Then —he admitted it to himself—he wanted to go home.

"Hey, Brann!" Suzanne ran up to stand beside him. "I saw you two. You had a fight, huuh? I bet you beat him good."

Brann looked up at her, puzzled.

"He doesn't usually fight. Usually he runs away. What made him fight? Was it you against him or the two of you against somebody else?"

Brann tried to think about what to say.

She didn't care what he had to say. "Are you going to come with me?"

"Where?"

"I told you, swimming. Mrs. Grynowski doesn't keep much of an eye on us, she's in ironing and listening to the radio. Do you dare? Or not."

"What about Kevin?"

"He's a sissy. He won't come."

"Are you sure it's all right?" Brann asked. A swim would feel even better than a shower.

She looked scornful. "Of course, it's not all right. But we can get away with it. Or are you a sissy too?"

Brann didn't even answer that. She was stupid to think he couldn't see through that kind of a trick. "I'm waiting for Kevin."

"Then you'll do it."

"I haven't said I'll do anything," Brann snapped at her. But why not? he asked himself. Kevin stepped out and Brann said quickly, "She knows about the fight, but I'm not planning to give her any details. Are you?"

Slowly, Kevin shook his head. His eyes moved to Suzanne's face, then back to Brann's.

"We're going swimming," Suzanne told her brother. "Without you."

"Hold on," Brann pitched in. "I didn't say that. Do you want to come, Kevin?"

Kevin didn't want to, Brann could see that. "I'm going," Brann said. Suzanne grinned at Kevin.

"Then I'll come with you," Kevin said. "It's hot enough. If you're lying though, Suzanne, if they haven't gone away, if we get caught—"

"What'll you do?" She sneered.

They walked through the small town, down its one main street. Everything was quiet. It was as if the heat hung so low it could squash even the buildings down. The stores had their doors open, and huge ceiling fans moved the sticky air around from outside to inside.

After they had passed through the town they began going up a long, steep hill. They walked on the shoulder of the winding road. No cars passed them, not going up away from the river valley, not going down toward the town. Woods grew to the very edges of the road, and leafy branches hung over it. Bushy undergrowth crowded up at the trunks of the trees.

The three children walked on uphill. When they had gone more than a mile, Brann finally asked how much farther it was. Suzanne had been waiting for this question. "Only another mile," she said. "Why? You tired?"

Brann denied it. His whole body was getting a layer of sweat over the previous layers. His T-shirt was soaked with it. He could feel the cuts on his right heel. But it felt good to be hot and tired, with the sharp pain of the cut reminding him that he was alive. It would feel good to jump into the water of a swimming pool.

At the crest of the hill you could look down along three roads. Each road wound off and away, but not before revealing a glimpse of mansions between tree trunks.

Brann knew a mansion when he saw one. A mansion was big and spread out, so that you knew there were bedrooms for a dozen people. A mansion was built out of fancy materials, gray stone or long white clapboards or yellow brick. A mansion sat on its site proudly, and its lawn stretched away from it like the cloth beneath a Christmas tree. A mansion looked rich. These were mansions.

Suzanne led them into a patch of woods growing wild. At the end of it, in a small dell at the bottom of a sloping lawn, a long blue rectangle of water waited.

Brann stood at the edge of the lawn and looked up the slope to where the house stood. The house had one large central section and two long wings. Each wing was about four times as big as Brann's own house. Two broad stone staircases, one at either side of the lawn, curved down from the house to the pool. The same stone had been used to make a patio area around the pool.

"It's like a movie set," Brann said.

"So what?" Suzanne asked.

Brann ignored her and turned to Kevin. The boy

nodded, his gray eyes roaming along the lines of the house. "Because of the proportions, can you see it?" Brann could see; his father had taught him about proportion. He wondered who had taught Kevin. Kevin talked on: "If it was one story higher, or lower, it would be all wrong, unsymmetrical. Even if it matched perfectly. And it doesn't look heavy, does it? Those big windows all along the ground floor, they keep it from looking heavy."

"How'd you like to live in a house like that?" Brann asked. He could almost taste the pleasure it would give him.

Kevin shrugged. "I don't know. But I'd like to build one. We could make one with the—"

"Are we going to swim or stand around?" Suzanne interrupted. She stripped down to her underpants.

The place looked deserted enough. They left their clothes in the woods and ran barefoot across the grass. The water, blue and cooler than the sky, was glassy-still. They hesitated at the deep end.

"I don't think—" Kevin began, in a whisper.

Brann fell into the water. He let himself sink and sink into its wetness and coolness, absorbing it into every pore of his whole body. He expelled the air from his lungs to keep himself going down, floating down, alone in the watery world. When he felt the bottom under his hands and knees, he opened his eyes and swam underwater until the need for air forced him up. Then he pushed hard with his feet against the bottom and shot up, spattering fat drops of water around him. He shook his hair out of his eyes and dived down under-water again.

Out of the corner of his eye he could see the air bubbles of the two other swimmers. He ignored them. The water washed at his skin, cleaning it. In the pools near Brann's house, or the motel pools he'd swum in, he'd gotten a lot of practice swimming underwater, because you could go your own way no matter how crowded the pool was. The bottom of this pool was painted bright blue and made of rough cement, not the usual plastic liner. The temperature was cooler than Brann was used to because, he guessed, the pool wasn't heated. There was no chlorine to burn at his eyes. But the liquidity all around him, and the silence pressing on his ears, and the blurred outlines of everything, those he recognized.

Brann surfaced again and looked around. Suzanne was on the diving board, bouncing. Kevin did a dog paddle down at the shallow end. Brann rolled onto his back and floated.

He saw a deep blue sky onto which marched high-headed white clouds. This was ringed by the leafy tops of trees and the tall roof of the house. He heard insects chirping and buzzing and whirring, all around. He heard Suzanne dive into the water and the plashing sound as the waves she made hit the sides of the pool.

Brann knew the two Connell children were in the pool with him, but he felt alone. The deep, luxurious sense of privacy, of solitude, seeped inside of him, as gentle as water. He had never felt this way before. But then, he realized, he'd never been alone before in quite this way. Some of it was the cultivated beauty of the setting: the pool, the green and empty lawn, the well-made house, the trees grown tall over the many years, the deep sky. Some of it was the queer place in time he now occupied, not really himself, unable to be really anyone else. Some of it was reaction to the caves. And some of it, maybe the most important part, was the way for the first time in his life he was in a place where there was more than enough room outside, so that he could stretch inside and see how much room there was in there, and how much of him there was in there to fill the outside spaces.

What kind of thinking was that? Brann asked himself. He grinned up into the sky: the kind of thinking you did when your brain got so scared it split. No big deal. He rolled over and did a crawl up and down the pool, ending up next to Kevin. He started a ducking and pulling game. Suzanne swam down and joined in, but she always took Brann's side against Kevin and the game was no longer fun. Brann pulled himself up out of the pool. He sat with his legs hanging over the deep water, kicking gently. Kevin came to sit beside him. They dripped together in cool, companionable silence.

"You know what I like?" Brann said at last. "The privacy. At home, I don't even have my own room that I share with some one person. I sleep in a den that's used during daytime and nighttime. School is crowded. Beaches are crowded."

"But you said—" Kevin interrupted. He stopped himself and stared at Brann, squinting into the sunlight, his crew cut spiking out of his head. Brann didn't say anything; he just sat quiet while Kevin stared and thought. "Do you have anyplace to go?" Kevin asked at last. And that was the home question, Brann thought, the question at the heart of it.

"It's OK—I hope," Brann answered. He continued trying to figure out something he had just understood, because that was more interesting right now than his problems. "Stores are crowded too. Streets are crowded. Here"—the idea took him away into a surprising direction—"do you think it drives people crazy being crowded all the time? This privacy—you know?—I'd be willing to rob a bank, or cheat someone, or almost anything, if I could get enough money to buy a place like this. And I'm not even dishonest. Imagine how tempting it would be, if you weren't honest to begin with. I never thought about that before."

"You don't have to be rich to get privacy," Kevin pointed out. "Uncle Andrew's not rich and his farm has this same feeling. Of course, it's not beautiful, not like this. But who cares about that?"

"I do," Brann started to say. Then he stopped. Because he didn't, he really didn't; and he hadn't known that before about himself. It wasn't the fancy house or the close-cropped, well-watered lawn. It was the space and silence, and the sense that they were the only ones here.

"You're right," he said instead. He looked at Kevin's gray eyes, trying to see inside the boy, this strange kid who seemed to understand already things Brann was just starting to figure out.

Suzanne paddled up to them and suggested a race. Brann had watched these children swim. "You two go ahead and I'll be the starter. Twice up and back?"

"I can't swim that far," Kevin objected.

"OK, once up and back."

"And you'll race the winner," Suzanne announced.

They started at the deep end, each hanging on with one hand. "Ready? Set? Go!" Brann called. Lazily, he watched them swim. Kevin had a dogged half-crawl, and his feet sent up great splashes of water. His kick was rotten. Suzanne flailed her arms and her legs, making up in energy for all that she lacked in skill. She looked like a windup toy, splashing, splashing, lifting her head straight up to get a breath and check on Kevin's position. They didn't know how to make a racing turn, either. Brann stood and watched this, wondering whether when his turn came he should swim as well as he could (which wasn't that well, but was miles better than Kevin) or rein himself back just because he was so much better. He heard a dog barking, but he couldn't even tell what direction the distant voice came from, because the hills and trees distorted sound. The dog didn't sound alarmed.

As the racers came back up the length of the pool, Suzanne pulled steadily ahead. Her arms rotated into and out of the water, like windmill arms. Her face— eyes and open mouth—gleamed with victory. She won by six strokes.

"I get to rest before I race you," she said to Brann. She hung onto the edge of the pool and gasped for breath. "He's no race at all."

"Fine by me," Brann agreed. "I want a fair race," he said, adding silently to himself, "So I can beat you to hell and back and there'll be no excuses." He leaned down to give Kevin a hand, pulling him up out of the water.

"Nobody beats Suzanne. No matter how good you are, she wants to win so bad she just does it."

"Which some people never seem to learn," she said to Kevin. She grinned up at Brann, "But some people are born stupid."

Brann began to be eager for this race.

He started, like Suzanne, from the side of the pool. He went down the length, taking it easy, with long, regular strokes and quick butterfly kicks. He breathed every four strokes. He came to the end two strokes ahead of her and didn't do a racing turn but touched the end and turned around on the surface of the water. Then, passing her on his second stroke out, as she went in to touch the wall, he turned it on. He kicked at maximum efficiency, from the ankles. He breathed only every seventh stroke. He drove his arms into the water as strongly as he could without sacrificing rhythm. He hadn't hurried the first lap, so he had all of his best energy to put into the second. He cut through the water like a power boat, delighting in the sense of his own muscles working, in the smooth stretch and pull, in the swift, clean movement. When he turned his head to breathe, he could see no sign of Suzanne.

At the end of the pool, Brann grabbed the edge and grinned up at Kevin. Only Kevin wasn't there.

Surprised, Brann hoisted himself and looked across the lawn. Kevin was running into the woods.

Brann turned around and saw Suzanne struggling to free herself from the grip of a short dark-haired man who leaned over into the pool and held onto one of her arms.

"Lemme go! Are you deaf? Let me go!" she shrieked.

Brann hesitated between the girl and the woods.

As long as the man was holding Suzanne, Brann could make it to the woods. But you didn't go off and leave someone else in trouble. Did you?

Why not? She'd been asking for trouble all day.

Yeah, but you didn't. Brann had no choice.

He walked slowly down alongside the pool. The man was wearing an undershirt, a pair of baggy denim overalls, and heavy shoes without socks. His hair was slicked down.

"I'll tell my father!" Suzanne cried. "He'll have something to say to you! You better be careful around my father!"

The man took one look at Brann and nodded his head, in greeting. Then he lifted Suzanne up, out of the pool and onto the stones. He was strong enough, Brann thought. He kept his grip on her arm.

"What names are you?" he demanded. He spoke his words thickly, as if his mouth was full of potatoes.

"Suzanne Connell," she said, bold. "And my father's Thomas Connell, the builder. You better let me go now."

The man held on and looked at Brann.

"Brann with two n's," Brann said.

"Brann what?"

"Connell," Brann said, before he thought. Suzanne flashed her eyes at him, but she didn't say anything. A mean little smile turned up the corners of her mouth, as if she and Brann shared a secret, and she knew more about the secret than Brann did.

"Suzanne and Brann," the man said. "Good. We will be going down and seeing just what your great father says. Your friend has made a getaway, but you have not been so lucky."

"He's a chicken," Suzanne muttered.

Brann didn't argue with her. He was disappointed. Not angry at Kevin, just disappointed. It was too bad the kid was the way he was, in that way. That wasn't all there was, but that part was—too bad.

"You have been trespassing on private property. That breaks the law," the man said. "We will go ask your father what he thinks about trespassing on private property."

"You can't take us home." Suzanne sounded scared. Why should she be scared? "We won't ever do it again. Honest. I promise. Please mister—you don't have to tell him."

The man studied her until she finally stopped. "I do yes have to tell him. And this makes some importance to you. Good. You got clothes somewhere? You, Brann, get them. Then follow up this way." He indicated with his free hand the far wing of the house. "My truck waits for you there. You will not fear the dog barking, for he is enchained."

"You gonna run away too?" Suzanne demanded. "I'll tell anyway, you can bet your boots." Brann didn't bother to answer her.

They rode down the long, winding hill in a pickup truck. Suzanne tried everything to talk the caretaker out of taking them home. Then she tried to talk him out of telling her father. Her father, she said, wouldn't be home yet anyway, and he wouldn't like being called away from work.

The caretaker said he didn't believe Suzanne. Then, he said, he knew of Thomas Connell, and Thomas Connell would think this was important, his children trespassing on private property.

Brann put his shirt on in the kitchen. Suzanne sat at the table, shivering. The caretaker dialed the number written by the telephone. "They come home right away," he announced to the children, and sat down to wait.

Kevin padded into the room. His hair was still wet although his overalls were dry. "You are the other one?" the caretaker asked.

Kevin nodded, dumb and pale.

"You should have stayed getawayed," the caretaker remarked. "If you run away you can stay away just as easy."

"I should've been the one to stay, Brann," Kevin said. "I'm sorry."

"That's OK," Brann said. He hadn't expected Kevin to come back so soon. He hadn't expected Kevin to come back at all. You had to respect the kid.

After a while, Mr. and Mrs. Connell came in the door. Thomas Connell's face was dark with anger, his footsteps heavy. He shook the caretaker's hand and they went out onto the porch to talk.

In the kitchen, nobody spoke. Suzanne was crying and sniveling. Kevin's mouth was tight at the corners. When Mr. Connell came back inside alone, Mrs. Connell looked at him. Her face looked simply tired.

"Take the boys to the living room, Polly. I'll begin with Suzanne."

He took the belt off of his pants. It was a wide, black leather belt, with a heavy brass buckle on one end. When he had it off, he slapped it once on the table.

Suzanne began to cry out loud.

Brann and Kevin went into the dim living room to wait their turns.

six

EVENING light washed over the living room. Long golden bars of sunlight slipped under the lowered shades.

Kevin stood by the dining room door, listening anxiously to the wails and carryings-on from the kitchen. Brann went to look out a window. He snapped up the shade, then remembered that he should have asked Mrs. Connell first. When he turned to ask permission, he saw that she was sitting in a polished wooden rocker. Her belly ballooned out before her. She leaned her head back and closed her eyes.

Suzanne shrieked so loudly he could hear every word, every cry, even though the dining room was between them. Her father told her to take down her pants, and she shrieked that she was a girl so he better be careful with her, and that it was all Kevin's idea. She yelled for her mother. "I don't want to be whipped!"

she cried. Then she sobbed it over and over. "I don't want to! It's not fair—they made me! I don't want to be whipped!"

"Lean over the chair, let's get this over with."

"No! No!" shrieked Suzanne, but she must have obeyed, because then Brann heard the slap of the belt against bare flesh. "OWWWW! That hurts! That's enough! Owww! No more, please, Daddy!" The belt fell again. Three strokes in all.

If he went out the front door, Brann thought, he would never be able to come back in, and he would never be able to return to his own house, to his own parents. He heard Kevin make a little whimpering sound.

Mrs. Connell spoke without opening her eyes. "I don't know why you did something like that. You get no sympathy from me."

Kevin gulped and was silent.

Suzanne came out from the kitchen. Her face was wet with tears, but she was smiling. "You're next," she told Kevin. She looked over at Brann and the smile stayed on her face. When Kevin went into the kitchen, she stood listening at the door.

Kevin didn't talk to his father. He apparently lowered his pants right away. Brann heard the belt crack against Kevin's skin. Once, twice, three times— then again and again. At the sixth stroke, Kevin howled, and at the seventh.

Kevin stood in the dining room doorway, his chest heaving, his eyes watering. His fathomless gray eyes met Brann's and Brann nodded.

Mr. Connell waited by the kitchen table, with a

chair before him. Brann guessed he was supposed to drape his arms over the back of the chair and stick his backside out.

"Take down your pants," Mr. Connell said. He didn't even sound angry. He didn't even sound as if he cared about what he was doing.

"No," Brann said, quiet.

"You're a guest in my house, you follow our rules," Mr. Connell said.

"Yes sir," Brann answered. "I can understand that. But I won't take down my pants." He couldn't have taken them down and bent over. That—that wasn't something anybody should be able to make you do.

Mr. Connell studied him, as if assessing how scared he was. Well, he was scared enough, Brann thought. Mr. Connell's little eyes grew angry. "Should I send you home for your father to whip you?" he threatened.

Brann glared back at him. "My father doesn't whip me," he said, suddenly proud. "My father wouldn't do that to his kids."

The man growled. "Bend over."

Brann bent his head and shoulders over the back of the wooden chair. He concentrated on the muddy brown linoleum floor beyond the chair seat. He focused his eyes on a puddly spot under the table.

The belt fell, and he gasped. It really hurt. A split second after the sound, the pain began. It fell again and Brann heard a little protesting sound escape from his lips. This time it had fallen partly across the tops of his legs.

He bit on his lip. He couldn't focus his mind on

100

anything, but he could keep silent. Mr. Connell was whipping so hard you could hear him grunt. Three, four.

Brann bit down hard and squeezed his eyes closed. Five. His body trembled and he couldn't stop it. He made a picture for his mind, of the bright hot air and the cool green of the trees around the swimming pool. Inside his mind, he dived into the pool and floated all alone, in the cool blue underwater.

Six. Wait. Seven. Brann tasted blood. Eight. He made himself think cool and blue, while telling himself it couldn't last forever. Kevin got seven. Why should Brann get more? Nine. It had to end soon. Unless the belt would keep falling until Brann cried. If he howled, would that stop Mr. Connell? Ten. Brann waited.

It was over.

"Get up now," Mr. Connell ordered. Brann opened his eyes and stood straight, facing the man. His legs quivered, but he made his face stay quiet. Mr. Connell was looking at him oddly. "You're the oldest, you should have stopped them," he said.

Brann could have argued, but he just nodded his head instead. His mouth was filling with blood, and he swallowed it. He guessed he'd bit through his lip.

"You said you were one of mine. That was a lie," Mr. Connell said.

"Yes, it was." Brann stared back at the man, thinking his own thoughts about that.

After a while Mrs. Connell called out, "Andrew's here," and Mr. Connell told Brann to wait in the living room. Brann didn't look around him as he walked out and stood by a window.

"You didn't have to take down your pants," Suzanne said in her normal voice. "You got it easy."

"Shut up, Suzanne," Brann said, without turning around. He didn't know how Kevin could stand it, with this horrible sister and that father and his mother who didn't even act like a human being.

"It's not usually this bad," Kevin said. "Brann?"

"It's OK," Brann said. "I'm just angry."

Kevin came to stand beside him. "Angry? Why? They're right. We were trespassing."

"That's not it," Brann said. It was fair enough to be whipped, he guessed. "It's the way he does it." He didn't like to think about all the long years Kevin Connell had lived in this family.

"It's the only way he knows," Kevin said. "It's because he's scared."

"*He's* scared?" Brann snorted.

They were called into the kitchen. Suzanne plopped herself down into a chair and sat with her hands folded on the table in front of her, looking like a perfect angel. Brann and Kevin stood. Brann knew how much it would hurt to sit down.

A tall, thin man sat with Mr. and Mrs. Connell at the table. His hair was thick and white, his face was tanned red-brown, and his black eyes snapped with life. Kevin looked across at him and the man winked. Kevin's whole face lit up. His broad mouth stretched into a smile that was about the happiest thing Brann had ever seen. There was no sadness to this smile.

They all seemed to have forgotten that Brann was there. Nobody introduced him, nobody looked at him. The man, Uncle Andrew, if Kevin's expression was any clue, sat across the table from where Kevin and Brann stood. "And how's the world with you, lad?" he asked Kevin.

Kevin didn't answer, just smiled and nodded.

"I've been talking to your uncle," Mr. Connell said. "Look at me when I'm speaking to you, boy."

Kevin's eyes turned reluctantly to his father.

"Billy will go to the farm this summer. You'll stay here and work for me. You'll be here to help your mother with the new baby."

Kevin fell absolutely still. Brann didn't dare look at him.

"But why?" Kevin asked.

"It's your responsibility. You can begin to learn my business."

Kevin bolted around the table and grabbed his uncle's brown hand. Uncle Andrew looked at Mr. Connell, his eyes laughing as if to say, Didn't I tell you so?

"But why?" Kevin asked his uncle.

"It's what your father says, lad. It's what he said to me, I'm lucky to get the free labor."

"But you said—" Kevin protested. "You said I was the best worker you'd ever had. You said you didn't know how the farm would do without me."

Brann sucked at his lower lip. It had stopped bleeding, but the taste of blood was still in his mouth.

"You know how I blather, lad. Not that it's a lie, you've done a man's work, more than my boys ever did at your age, and with a better heart for it. But a man blathers and sings and tells stories—and he can't be held accountable for everything he says."

Kevin clung to his uncle's hand. "But you said you couldn't imagine a summer without me coming to help out. And he doesn't like having me around and you said you did."

"It's all decided," Mr. Connell said.

"But what if I don't want to?" Kevin demanded desperately.

"What?" Anger turned Mr. Connell's face red.

"I don't want to work for you. You never said I'd have to work for you. You never said I had to stop going to the farm."

"That's enough," Mrs. Connell spoke. Her eyes were not angry, just tired. "There'll be no more out of you."

"Didn't I warn you, Thomas?" Uncle Andrew asked. Then he laughed, easily, and looked up at Kevin's face. "It's not the end of the world, lad. Look at it this way, life has its ups and it has its downs. Right now, you're in what you might call a down." Kevin nodded agreement. "That's better now. What I say to myself, from the bottom of the pit, looking up, you might say, at the stars or at the sun, I tell myself: Lay low until life gets back to an up."

"Does that mean I'll be able to come back next summer?" Kevin asked.

Even Brann knew that wasn't what the man meant. What the man meant was that there wasn't anything he was going to do for Kevin.

But Uncle Andrew burst out laughing, as if that was the funniest thing he'd heard. "What a lad," he said. "What a lad."

"Does it?" Kevin insisted.

"No, it doesn't, so set your mind at rest about that," Kevin's father said.

"And do you know anyone can talk Thomas Connell out of anything he's made his mind up to?" Uncle Andrew asked his nephew, with an easy smile.

Brann saw Kevin curl back up into himself. Then he made one last try. "But you didn't ask me." Big tears spilled out of his eyes. "You didn't even *ask* me what I wanted to do."

"What children want can't be counted," Mrs. Connell said. "It's enough trouble keeping them fed and clothed."

Kevin ran out of the room. Brann heard him pounding up the stairs. He didn't know what he was supposed to do, and he was busy trying to swallow past a lump in his throat. Whether the lump was sadness for Kevin or anger at Uncle Andrew and the Connells, Brann couldn't tell.

Mr. Connell stood up. "I could use a beer," he said. "Andrew?"

"A cool beer would not come amiss."

"Then we'll be back in a while," Mr. Connell told his wife.

"I'll have supper waiting." She watched them leave, then pushed her hands on the table top to stand up. "You, Brann," she said. "There's peanut butter and bread. I'm going to fetch the children home, if you'd make up a plate of sandwiches. I don't know how long that boy will sulk in his room—the old people need their tray. They won't like it but pay them no mind."

Brann nodded. He watched her leave, watched the door swing closed behind her, watched her descend the steps with one hand on the railing.

"I'm hungry," Suzanne said.

Brann made her a peanut butter sandwich and poured her a glass of milk. Then he made six more sandwiches, four on a plate for Kevin's grandparents, two for Kevin. He put three glasses of milk on the tray. He turned on the light, put the heel of the loaf back into the breadbox, capped the peanut butter and lay the spreading knife in the sink. He looked at Suzanne. She stuck out her tongue at him.

"When you finish, wash and dry your dishes and go to bed," he told her. She looked like she wanted to say no, but didn't dare. "Whether it's early or not," Brann said, because he knew what she'd say next. "Or you can go out—and get yourself killed or something. I don't really care a bit."

He heard what he had said. One day with these people and already he was changed by them. How did Kevin stand it?

Brann was stopped by a sudden cold thought: Kevin stood it because he wasn't like them; but Brann was enough like them for them to have an effect on him. He didn't want to be like them. He wanted to be like Kevin—not exactly like, of course—but not like them. He picked up the tray. "Leave the light on for when your parents get back. OK?" Suzanne didn't answer.

Brann carried the tray carefully up the two flights of stairs, watching the milk to keep down the sloshing. Before he went into Kevin's room, he took a plate and two glasses down the hall. Kevin's grandfather stood alone in the sitting room down the hall, looking out the window, his back straight. "I've brought your supper," Brann said loudly.

"No need to shout. I can hear you," the man answered, without turning around.

Brann took the tray to Kevin's door. It was closed. He knocked. "It's me—Brann."

There was no answer. He balanced the tray on one hand and turned the knob.

Kevin was lying on his back on the bed. He didn't bother to look at Brann. Brann put the tray down at the foot of the bed and looked at the boy. His light, spiky hair and his expressionless face and his deep gray eyes —Brann saw them all. He had seen them before, too, on his father.

"Buck up," Brann said, as his mother often said to him. "How bad can it be, after all?"

An unwilling half-smile moved Kevin's mouth. "Couldn't be much worse," he answered. He was holding a scrunched-up piece of paper.

"Could too," Brann said, still sounding like his mother. "Look, I made peanut butter sandwiches. You want one?"

Kevin sat up. He dropped the paper onto the floor. It was his picture of Uncle Andrew's farm. "Yeah," he said. "I'm hungry. I wish I wasn't. I thought that what I had to do was stand up for what I wanted. I wish I hadn't—"

Brann sat gently on the bed facing him. "Never mind wishes," he advised, biting into one of the sandwiches.

"You're braver than I'll ever be," Kevin said. He

began to take an interest in the conversation and to chew hungrily. "You kept your pants on. I didn't think he'd let you."

"He had to," Brann said, pleased with himself now that he was remembering it.

"Why?"

"Fate," Brann said. He changed the subject. "What did you mean your father is scared?"

"What's it matter. Anyway."

"I can't figure it out," Brann admitted. "It seems to be he's got everyone pretty scared of him."

"Even Uncle Andrew," Kevin agreed.

"Do you think," Brann asked, "that he minded because you like your uncle better than him?"

The gray eyes looked at him, sad. "Naw. He doesn't think much of me, or of Uncle Andrew. He's not scared like that. He's scared that if he ever stops working, he'll lose the business. If there aren't any jobs. Before we came here, and when he was out of work— and he's scared that if he lets up for a second it'll all happen again. I guess I can understand that."

"Do you really have to work for him?"

"What else can I do? If Uncle Andrew doesn't want me on the farm. Anyway."

"You could refuse. You could run away."

"Can't," Kevin said. "Besides, my mother's going to have that baby and I'll have to be in charge here. There isn't anything to do. It's just as bad for them as for me. But it doesn't seem right, because we were so glad to move here. At first. But things change and people change to go with the things. I don't know. But there isn't anything I can do. Even if there was—but they need me here and I have to be where I'm needed. Even if I'm no good at it."

Brann knew Kevin was right, but he couldn't accept that. Kevin could, he realized. Kevin could accept losing his summer at the farm and being hammered on and taking care of the little kids and being whipped that way; and he didn't even get angry. It was giving up, in a way, but it was something more too. Brann had a glimpse, just a vague idea, of the kind of courage Kevin had. Courage for facing the truth, inside himself.

Brann didn't know if he had that kind of courage. In fact, he was pretty sure he didn't, but he hoped he could learn it. And add it to the kind of courage he did have.

"Listen," Brann said, moving the tray down onto the floor, "I have an idea. You'll think I'm crazy, but listen." Kevin lay back and folded his arms behind his head, his face blank. "I have an idea that this baby isn't going to be a boy at all. It's going to be a girl, and you're going to like her, and she's going to like you, and you're going to be friends, all of your lives."

Kevin closed his eyes and shook his head slowly, from side to side. "You are crazy."

"Maybe," Brann allowed, "maybe. But I'll tell you what. Don't say anything, don't even think anything, but if it's a girl and they name her Rebecca—then I'm right."

"Anything you say," Kevin said, his voice sleepy.

"You'll remember?"

"I'll remember everything about today. Except for meeting you, it's been the worst day in my whole life."

"If I was you I'd forget today," Brann advised.

Kevin lay silent for a long time. "I guess so," he finally said. "What about you? Nothing's changed for you, has it? Whatever was wrong before, when you came in last night, is still wrong. Do you want me to help? Do you want to tell me? I don't know what I could do, but there might be something."

Brann looked at Kevin's face, the eyes closed, the mouth half open. "Tell you what—if I'm still here tomorrow, then I will. OK?"

"OK," Kevin said. "If you lived here you'd be my friend, wouldn't you?"

Brann nodded and then remembered that Kevin couldn't see him in the dark room, with his eyes closed. "Yeah," he said. "I guess so." It was the truth after all.

He sat and thought how funny that was. Then, when he saw that Kevin was asleep, he got up off the bed. Quietly, he kneeled down by the block fortress, the castle close, and dismantled the central building. Careful not to knock anything down, careful to do it exactly the same way, he crawled through the large gateway and curled up within the wall of building blocks, with the wooden floor under his shoulder. He was pretty tired himself. He could feel sleep creeping up to him like a wave on the incoming tide. For a minute, before losing consciousness, he felt a pinprick of fear: what if this wouldn't take him back? This fear hurt him deeper than the belt could begin to reach. Kevin didn't know how deep down inside frightened Brann could be. Or maybe he did. That was Brann's last thought before he slept.

Seven

□□□□□□□□□□□□□□□□□□□□□□□□□□

BRANN opened his eyes to a bright yellow light. Sunlight. He snapped his eyes shut.

It hadn't worked. He was still here. There. Then. He had been so sure that the blocks were the way back, but he had been wrong. A knot of panic contracted his body. What could he do? What terrible thing had happened to him?

His brain was frozen and didn't work. He wanted, desperately, to go back to sleep. He didn't want to have to think about what had happened to him, or what he should do. He was absolutely and entirely alone for all of his life now. Who would be Brann Connell then, his friend Kevin's third child when Kevin grew up? Would Brann just be erased from the future? If he told Kevin what had really happened, would Kevin believe him?

This should have happened to Kevin, Brann thought to himself, trying to force himself back into the unconsciousness of sleep and out of this sun-brightened room. Kevin had the kind of courage to accept it.

The floor was hard under his shoulder. His body was stiff. In the background, he heard an unfamiliar sound, a smooth, sliding noise. Probably Mrs. Connell was sweeping the floors of the hallway. What would she say when she saw him still there? Brann wondered if he would live with the Connells now or go to an orphanage. His father never said anything about an orphan coming to live with them. Brann hoped he could be better at being a friend to Kevin Connell than he'd been at being a son.

He knew he had to open his eyes and deal with what had happened. Somehow. Kevin would help him.

He opened his eyes. He saw the wall of the castle close. The blocks had turned golden with the oils of many hands.

And Kevin's blocks were almost white, because they were new.

Brann twisted around onto his back. His feet knocked over walls and towers. He didn't notice that. He noticed instead, all at the same time, the damp cellar cement underneath him, the one yellow lightbulb in the center of the ceiling, and his father, Kevin Connell, forty-seven years old, his wide mouth tight at the corners after the morning argument with his wife. Brann's father was planing down a long piece of dark-grained wood. The shavings curled off the top of the plane with a smooth, sliding sound.

His father lifted his head and looked at Brann. He smiled. "I thought you'd sleep forever," he said. "Like King Arthur under the hill. To be reawakened in time of need." His eyes within thick black lashes were muddy gray and secretive.

Brann could have laughed aloud. He felt like yelling. Instead, he stretched out his arms and legs as far as they could reach. The fortress tumbled down on him. "Maybe," he said. "Maybe I did. Maybe I am."

He couldn't stop grinning. He was home.

He sat up, then stood up. His shoulders and legs hurt. "What day is it? What time is it?"

His father started planing again. "It's today, just like it was when you hid out down here. It must be near lunchtime. I've been down here—maybe an hour."

"Doing what?"

"Planing." His father didn't say anything else.

"What're you making?"

"Wood curlings," with a reluctant half-smile.

"But why did you marry her?" Brann would never have asked that question of his father, but he didn't remember that in time. It was a perfectly natural question to ask his friend Kevin.

"Well, I love her." His father's eyes were fixed on the smooth board. "She's got drive, and there's no one like her when she's happy. And she loves me."

"She yells at you. She hammers and hammers."

"She cares about us, and about herself too. She fights for herself—if you don't admire her—what she's accomplished—you're making a big mistake."

Brann had never thought about that.

"I guess I figured that with all of her ambition and energy, she'd keep me up to the mark," his father said. "I have a habit of letting things slide, and I thought she'd change that for me. But, nobody else can change you, that way. You've got to change things yourself. That's what I was just thinking about. You never knew your grandmother. My mother. Your mother is a lot like my mother, at least what I remember of her because I was pretty young when she died. In some ways they are very similar. She didn't let things slide, my mother."

"I guess not," Brann agreed, remembering.

"You don't have to humor me. It's OK. Anyway, anyway. It's fate and all that," Kevin Connell said. He continued planing.

Brann stood right up close beside his father. It took some getting used to, his father being older than him again, and bigger again. "What about this farm, Dad?"

"What about it? I want to keep it and your mother wants to sell it."

"No, I mean is it the one you used to work on with your uncle?"

"You know that."

"Is it big?"

"Big enough to keep us in essentials, food and clothes. Not much else though," Kevin Connell said.

"Is there a pond?"

"The Ohio River goes right past it—though you can't call that water. It's more like liquid sludge. I haven't seen it for, oh, almost thirty years, I guess. But it was bad the last time I was there. I don't like to think what that river looks like now. Or smells like. The farm has a couple of small creeks, no fishing streams, no swimming holes. Let's not talk about it, OK?"

"But how come you stopped going there?" Brann insisted.

114

"I started working for my father in the summers instead. I was ten or so. *That* I remember, because he just announced that I wasn't going back to the farm. I thought I'd die. But I didn't, as you see. I toted bricks and stirred mortar. I learned how to build things from my father, do repairs, and plumbing too. My father was a worker, and he worked me. My brothers too, when they got old enough."

"Did you do all right with him?" Brann asked.

His father shrugged.

"Dad? There are caves in that part of Pennsylvania, aren't there? Did you ever go spelunking?"

"Whatever makes you ask a question like that?"

"I dunno."

"You haven't been doing that with your friends, have you? You do know it can be dangerous. Have you?"

Brann was tempted to tell the story, to find out from his father's reaction if it had really happened. Then he remembered that he had promised never to tell—and he wanted to keep his promise to Kevin Connell. "No, I just wondered. I'm probably still half asleep." Maybe it *was* all a dream he'd had. Why should that make him feel disappointed? After all, how could he have traveled back thirty-seven years in time and been himself, his father's son, when his father was only ten years old. That was impossible.

"But it's funny," his father said. "Because I once had a nightmare about being lost in a cave. I can still taste the feeling of it—deep and dark, I don't know what made me have that nightmare. It's the only one I remember from when I was little. Kids have such vivid imaginations. Tell you what, maybe it really happened, and if it happened it was something I don't want to remember. But that's not the kind of thing you forget, is it?"

"I don't think so." So, Brann thought, it had all been a dream. All the things he dreamed hadn't really happened. The boy he'd spent that faraway day with hadn't been his father really. He rubbed his lower lip with his fingers, to keep his mouth from drooping down the way it wanted to. He grunted with surprised pain. His lower lip was swollen.

"Anything wrong? What happened to your lip, Brann? You look like somebody punched you."

Brann ran an experimental tongue over it. "Nobody punched me," he said. "It feels like I cut it, I wonder why—"

Then he knew why. And that was why his body was stiff, too, because it hadn't been a dream but a reality. Impossible, but real. There was one other way to check. "Dad? Why *did* you name me Brann? I mean, really why."

Kevin Connell put down his plane and looked at his red-haired son. "The truth is, I don't know. I honestly don't. I was all set to name you Thomas, we'd decided. Then the nurse brought you in and I saw you —I'd not seen you before, remember. I held you, all eight squalling pounds of you, and the name—came into my mind. Exactly the way I said, Brann with two n's. I didn't even know it was a genuine name until I looked it up later. It felt so right for you; it was the name you were supposed to have. It was your name. I'll tell you," Kevin Connell said, "it may sound crazy, but I had this feeling. I've had it a couple of times in my life—knowing what has to be. When your aunt Rebecca was born, I had it then. When I first met your mother. That feeling is a good sign, as I take it. And that is all the truth I know about your name."

Brann listened intently. When his father finished speaking, he bent his face down. He knew that his eyes were shooting gray lights out, and he didn't want his father to see. It *had* happened, but his father had forgotten all about it. That was OK. If his father had needed to remember, then he would have. There was no reason for Brann to try to remind him.

But how could a thing like that happen? If the Brann Brann was hadn't traveled back in time, then the Brann he was wouldn't have had his name. To be in either place, he had to be in both places. There was a hard-edged inevitability to it. Fate again.

"It doesn't make sense," he said.

Kevin Connell picked up the plane again, running his fingers over its cutting edge. "I don't much care about that. Do you?"

Brann threw his arms around his father and hugged him as hard as he could. He felt his father's big rib cage and broad shoulders. "What's that for?" Kevin Connell asked mildly, but he hugged Brann back and swatted at his backside affectionately.

Brann winced but he didn't draw away. "Because we're friends. Aren't we."

You didn't really know somebody unless you knew him when he was a kid. Kids didn't have so many walls built up around them, to hide behind and keep safe; kids hadn't built all those walls yet. They had some—

Brann had some, he knew that. But it was clearer with kids what they were really like. He could begin to know his father now.

"I guess so," Kevin Connell said. "I hope so." He rumpled Brann's hair.

Brann's father knew him, then, too, that way. Because Brann *was* a kid, his kid. Brann wondered what his father thought of him. He hoped his father respected him. He looked up at his father and stepped back.

"Listen, Dad?" The idea seemed to have been taking shape in his mind for a long time, but it was just now finished. "I've got an idea. No, listen, it's a good one."

"You sound like your mother."

"Well, I am," Brann answered. "In lots of ways. Now look—this farm. What if, instead of selling the farm, we sold this house? We could move to the farm, and Mom could go to law school out there. Isn't there a law school out there?"

"Probably. There's the University of Pittsburgh."

"Is it a good school?"

"Good enough. It's not New York good, I guess. But that's not Harvard good either, so who cares. And who knows, anyway. What do we know about stuff like that?"

His father was only half-listening, Brann knew, but he kept talking: "We could farm for a living, and the money from this house could send her to law school and Sarah to college too. Would there be enough?"

"Maybe. But what about you?"

"I keep telling you. I'm twelve, and that's too

young to begin worrying about college. Besides, Mom's so smart, she'll be through law school and raking in the money by the time my turn comes around."

Kevin Connell laughed. "Crafty. You're a crafty kid."

"Could we? Dad? Pay attention—could we do it?"

Kevin Connell studied his son's earnest face. "I don't know. I don't think so. Unless—you know Will Whitcomb?"

"Sure, Billy's father."

"I ran into him on the train one day—his car was in the shop or something. I was drawing something, I can't remember. He said—I ought to send the drawings to a publisher. He said publishers need people to do drawings and he thought mine were good enough."

"What did you say?"

"Nothing. What could I say?"

"And you didn't *do* anything either, did you? You never even told us. Why didn't you tell us?"

Kevin Connell shrugged. "People say things they don't mean. How could I tell about him? And I didn't want your mother on my back about that, too. It was quite a while ago. And he might be wrong."

"But if he did mean it and he isn't wrong, would that mean we could get along on the farm?"

"It might. I don't know anything about it, Brann. But if . . . Lord, I could quit that job. I thought I was there until I just died at my desk. I can't imagine not sitting at that desk." Brann's father smiled quietly. Then the smile faded. "It's a grade-A idea, son. But I can't do it."

"Why?"

"Your mother has her heart set on the New York law school. And she's right, the least I can do is sell the farm for her."

Brann thought about this. If it was him, and there was something he wanted, really wanted, like his mother wanted to be a lawyer—but he wouldn't want his father to be unhappy unless there wasn't any other way. He guessed his mother might feel the same way he did. He couldn't be sure, but he guessed; and he *was* pretty sure all of a sudden.

"That's not necessarily true," he told his father. "The *least* you can do is give her a chance to decide. C'mon, Dad, you can't give up on it without trying it."

"What if she says she doesn't like the idea?"

"Tell her it's fate."

"She won't buy that."

"Try her, Dad. Just try her. You can't tell, can you? Not until you try." Brann looked straight into his father's eyes, trying to persuade him.

Fate isn't what either of us thought it was, Brann said to himself, the idea going off inside of him like a sparkler. Fate wasn't a smothering pillow, and it wasn't a steel sword blade. Fate was possibilities, all the possibilities, even the impossible ones.

"Maybe," said Kevin Connell. "OK, I will. Right now. Might as well get it over with. But you've got to come stand behind me. It's your brainstorm after all." He led the way upstairs.

They found Brann's mother in the den/bedroom/ TV room, sitting at the desk, reading. They stood quietly until she looked up. Kevin Connell kept his hand on his son's shoulder, but whether it was to remind Brann to wait or to keep himself feeling brave, Brann couldn't tell. That was OK, Brann thought. He had this kind of courage in abundance.

When his mother looked up, he spoke quickly. "What if we sell this house and live on the farm?"

She shook her head and sighed.

"Then you could go to law school in Pittsburgh."

"I don't know anything about Pittsburgh," she said. "I'd have to commute."

"Dad's done that for years," Brann pointed out to her.

Anger flashed into her eyes. Well, it was true, he thought. The hand tightened on his shoulder, but he ignored it. "He has, and he never complained."

Her head bent down over the book and she put her fingers into the hair at the back of her head. When she lifted her face again, tears were on it. Kevin Connell put his other hand on her shoulder, but he didn't try to comfort her.

"You're right," she said to Brann. "I know that. Oh Brann—I shouldn't have talked that way this morning, and I'm sorry."

Brann knew what it took for her to say that. "It's OK. I understand."

"It's just that—I feel as if I have to choose between living a life that will make me happy and the one that will make your father happy."

Brann's father started to protest, but she stopped him. "You know that, Kev. You know what I mean."

Kevin Connell spoke to Brann instead: "I'm not much help to her."

Before Brann could say anything, she answered:

"But you are—in your own way. And we really do love each other," she said, then turned back to Brann. "I won't ever talk like that in front of you again, I promise."

He knew he could believe her.

"I just get so frustrated," she said. Then she told herself, "That's no excuse."

"Yes, it is," Kevin Connell said. "Brann understands."

Brann did, of course. He knew the kind of anger that makes you lash out one minute and then walk away the next. "Listen, if we sold this house and moved out there we'd have the extra money. Don't you see?"

"Of course, I see that, and if your father knew how to farm, but you don't know, either of you, how fast money goes and—"

"If you want it, if you want to go to law school, it's a way. A way where Dad wouldn't have to lose the farm. Because he really doesn't want to."

"I don't want to be a farmer's wife."

"What about what Dad wants?"

"Besides the money we'd need just to live on. It's three years, Brann. This house isn't worth all that much. I'm sorry, but—"

Brann interrupted to explain about what Mr. Whitcomb had told his father. So he thought she should think about it, really think about it.

"Kevin. Is that right? And he liked it? And you never told me."

Brann's father nodded.

"But why didn't you tell me? You know I've always thought you were really good. How long ago was this?"

"Months. Last winter or maybe fall."

"But weren't you even pleased? I am. I think it's absolutely wonderful." Her eyes flashed green lights, brightening the whole room. "You should have told me. Kevin? You *should* have. Why didn't you?"

"I'm sorry Di. I didn't think—it's nothing definite. It's just a chance and not even a good one. There are lots of people who can draw."

"I don't mind taking chances, Kev. You know that. Honestly, sometimes—"

Brann interrupted again. "Let's stick to the point here. What about it, Mom?"

She wasn't even looking at him.

"What about selling this house and living on the farm," Brann said patiently, explaining his idea all over again. "It would make Dad happy," he concluded.

"Would it?" she asked her husband.

"I don't know, Di. It's so risky, depending for an income on farming and drawing. I don't know whether I can—"

"But do you want to?" she demanded.

"Well yes, but—"

"But what?"

Brann couldn't believe his father was backing down now.

"But if it doesn't work, if I can't make enough, if nobody is interested in my drawings—I couldn't take being blamed for ruining everything, Di."

Brann's mother took a deep breath. "You have my

word," she promised him. Then she turned to Brann: "Your father—has a way of seeing home truths and looking them in the eye," she said—said proudly.

So she knew that too; Brann should have guessed.

"We could look at a map and see just how far it is from the farm to the university," he suggested.

When they had seen the map and Brann's mother had decided that with the money from this house they could afford a used car for her to commute in, she raised her final objection: "What about good schools for Brann?"

"I don't care how good the schools are. For Pete's sake, leave me alone not to care about what I don't care about. OK?"

"OK," his mother said. She held up her hands in a gesture of mock surrender. "OK. OK."

Kevin Connell moved fast, once his wife had said the idea was fine by her; that, in fact, all things considered, she thought it might prove a workable arrangement. "You'll make a great lawyer talking that way, everything so careful," he remarked as he picked up the phone to call a real estate agent.

"What if I flunk out?" she asked suddenly. Brann looked at her in alarm. He hadn't considered this possibility. "Well?" she asked him.

He shook his head at her, wondering if she was teasing. But she looked like she was testing him, not teasing.

"You won't," he said. He didn't even want to think what it would be like if she did. He made himself think about it. "But if you do, or if you change your mind—"

She whooshed out a mouthful of air to show how impossible that was.

"—then it'll be up to me to establish the family fortunes," Brann concluded.

"What about me?"

"It'll be all right, Dad won't mind and neither will I." Brann eyed his mother thoughtfully, considering the possibilities for her. "And you can learn to can tomatoes and put up preserves and milk the cows."

"I better not fail then," she said.

"Yeah," Brann agreed.

TWO MONTHS later they were living in the neglected farmhouse. Harry was back at college and Sarah was going to stay with her best friend's family for her senior year. ("I'll never make a hayseed," she'd said. "But it's what you all want so go ahead and do it. Really. I'll come for Christmas and check it out.")

Brann's father couldn't put crops in that late in the year, but he had bought some chickens and expected an apple harvest. Their lives formed a pattern. In the mornings, after early chores, Kevin Connell retired to a studio he had made for himself up in the attic, where the light was good for drawing. In the afternoons he worked at fixing up the house, windows, wiring, plumbing, bookshelves. Brann's mother had enrolled in law school and was just waiting to begin. To fill up the time before she started, she scrubbed down walls and applied fresh paint. As long as she could go to school, she said, she didn't care where she lived—especially if Kevin was happy.

Mostly, Brann thought, they were happy—in their own way, of course. But then, he was beginning to think that people could only be happy in their own ways, and there was no point in trying to change them. There were still fights, most of them Level One. His mother was a fighter, he guessed. That wasn't necessarily bad. She still hammered on his father, like when Kevin Connell thought some pictures weren't ready yet to send away to a publisher, although he couldn't say what it was he wanted to do to make them better. His wife gave him an earful about if he was going to drag her out here he had to try and keep trying, that was the deal, and he had to keep up his end of it.

Brann figured once his mother started school and knew what kind of people were there and what kind of work they'd expect of her, she'd feel easier and not have time to fret about how much work was accomplished each day. He hoped he himself would feel easier, once he'd started school and knew what he'd gotten himself into.

They'd only had one Level Two fight, and that was about his mother's car. Kevin Connell wanted his wife to buy a new car, which would cost thousands of dollars. She wanted to get an old VW bug she'd found in a used car lot. She said he'd never been able to manage money, and it was her decision. She said if he was going to foist off the financial affairs on her then he couldn't step in and mess up her arrangements. She said, she wished he'd learn to keep his nose out of business where he knew he wasn't of any use. Kevin Connell sat and agreed with her and apologized.

Brann stuck around for the fight, making himself

remain quietly at the table. He didn't take sides. He didn't even want to. He thought, to himself, probably his mother was right and they couldn't afford a new car.

"I understand, Di," his father said.

His mother's angry voice burst over the table. "No, you don't. You don't want to be bothered, and I don't blame you. But really, Kev, you have to be realistic about something."

"I am being realistic," Brann's father said. "You're going to be commuting almost a hundred miles a day, tired, and in bad weather too. I want you in the safest possible car," he said.

"But—"

Kevin Connell interrupted her. "I'm not going to give in on this one, Di. You matter too much to me."

Brann's mother looked down at her clenched hands. Brann studied his glass of milk. He thought maybe his father was right about this, after all.

"I don't see how we can afford it," his mother said. Her eyes were shooting out warm green lights.

"You'll figure out a way," her husband promised her.

She shook her head, doubting, but didn't stop smiling. "There goes your new bike, Brann."

Brann hadn't thought of that. He took a quick breath, swallowed, and said, "That's OK. I can wait."

BRANN'S DAYS slowly piled up, one after the other, making a design he couldn't yet figure out. He helped his parents when he could and stayed out of the way when he couldn't. He spent a lot of time alone. He wandered around the farm, savoring the solitude and

127

spaciousness of the acres of woodland, farmland, and orchard. The hills rolled one after the other, like waves frozen in mid-swell. The fields, which had been abandoned for so long, had made their own crops, sword grass and Queen Anne's lace, and bobbing black-eyed susans. Brann learned to drive the tractor and mowed down the grass that was choking the orchard, where the green apples had grown to the size of apricots. He worked on the vegetable garden, ripping out the overgrowth, turfing over the soil. He fed the chickens and remembered the picture he'd seen taped to Kevin Connell's bedroom door.

Brann spent hours, too, down by the river, just looking at it. Because the Ohio River was cleaner now than when he'd seen it last, thirty-seven years ago, two months ago. It wasn't perfect, it wasn't finished yet, but it had really started. That, he couldn't believe. The water was deep blue-green, and fish and turtles were living in it. Clean little waves lapped cheerfully at the steep banks. In all those years, the Ohio River had gotten better, not worse. It wasn't possible, but it had happened.